Dear Reader,

Welcome to Silhouette Desire and another month of sensual tales. Our compelling continuity DYNASTIES: THE DANFORTHS continues with the story of a lovely Danforth daughter whose well-being is threatened and the hot U.S. Navy SEAL assigned to protect her. Maureen Child's *Man Beneath the Uniform* gives new meaning to the term *sleepover!*

Other series this month include TEXAS CATTLEMAN'S CLUB: THE STOLEN BABY with Cindy Gerard's fabulous *Breathless for the Bachelor*. Seems this member of the Lone Star state's most exclusive club has it bad for his best friend's sister. Lucky lady! And Rochelle Alers launches a brand-new series, THE BLACKSTONES OF VIRGINIA, with *The Long Hot Summer,* which is set amid the fascinating world of horse-breeding.

Anne Marie Winston singes the pages with her steamy almost-marriage-of-convenience story, *The Marriage Ultimatum.* And in *Cherokee Stranger* by Sheri WhiteFeather, a man gets a second chance with a woman who wants him for her first time. Finally, welcome brand-new author Michelle Celmer with *Playing by the Baby Rules,* the story of a woman desperate for a baby and the hunky man who steps up to give her exactly what she wants.

Here's hoping Silhouette Desire delivers exactly what *you* desire in a powerful, passionate and provocative read!

Best,

Melissa Jeglinski

Melissa Jeglinski
Senior Editor, Silhouette Desire

Please address questions and book requests to:
Silhouette Reader Service
U.S.: 3010 Walden Ave., P.O. Box 1325, Buffalo, NY 14269
Canadian: P.O. Box 609, Fort Erie, Ont. L2A 5X3

Breathless for
the Bachelor

CINDY GERARD

Silhouette®

Desire

Published by Silhouette Books
America's Publisher of Contemporary Romance

Special thanks and acknowledgment are given to Cindy Gerard
for her contribution to the TEXAS CATTLEMAN'S CLUB:
THE STOLEN BABY series.

This book is dedicated to the wonderful women who made yet another
Texas Cattleman's Club series come alive in vivid and sparkling color.
Your talent and generosity are treasured gifts.
Stephanie Maurer—editor extraordinaire.
Sara Orwig, Laura Wright, Kathie DeNosky, Cathleen Galitz and Kristi Gold—
Authors extraordinaire.
My Stetson is off to all of you.

 SILHOUETTE BOOKS

ISBN 0-373-76564-9

BREATHLESS FOR THE BACHELOR

Copyright © 2004 by Harlequin Books S.A.

Visit Silhouette at www.eHarlequin.com

Printed in U.S.A.

Books by Cindy Gerard

Silhouette Desire

The Cowboy Takes a Lady #957
Lucas: The Loner #975
*The Bride Wore Blue #1012
*A Bride for Abel Greene #1052
*A Bride for Crimson Falls #1076
†The Outlaw's Wife #1175
†Marriage, Outlaw Style #1185
†The Outlaw Jesse James #1198
Lone Star Prince #1256
In His Loving Arms #1293
Lone Star Knight #1353
The Bridal Arrangement #1392
The Secret Baby Bond #1460
Taming the Outlaw #1465
The Librarian's Passionate Knight #1525
Tempting the Tycoon #1539
Breathless for the Bachelor #1564

*Northern Lights Brides
†Outlaw Hearts

CINDY GERARD

Since her first release in 1991 hit the national #1 slot on the Waldenbooks bestseller list, Cindy Gerard has repeatedly made appearances on several bestseller lists, including *USA TODAY*. With numerous industry awards to her credit—among them the Romance Writers of America's RITA® Award and the National Reader's Choice Award—this former Golden Heart Finalist and repeat Romantic Times nominee is the real deal.

Cindy and her husband, Tom, live in the Midwest on a minifarm with quarter horses, cats and two very spoiled dogs. When she's not writing, she enjoys reading, traveling and spending time at their cabin in northern Minnesota unwinding with family and friends. Cindy loves to hear from her readers and invites you to visit her Web site at www.cindygerard.com.

"What's Happening in Royal?"

NEWS FLASH, February—These days Royal is losing eligible bachelors faster than you can say Jiminy Cricket! First David Sorrenson fell head over heels for the nanny he hired, then Clint Andover lip-locked with Nurse Roberts and now Travis Whelan settled down to be a family man with Natalie Perez and their infant daughter! Locals are taking bets as to who might be the next gent to take the plunge....

Could it be Dr. Nathan Beldon? As the new guy in town, Beldon is something of a mystery, but he's certainly handsome enough! And even though he hasn't been all that friendly with the locals, rumor has it that Trav's sister Carrie was spotted at Royal Diner on a date with the secretive doctor. Has Carrie set her sights on Dr. Beldon? if so, the good doctor is going to find himself in hot water when her overprotective brother finds out....

The real question is *why* is Carrie making eyes at Nathan Beldon when she's got a gorgeous hunk like Ry Evans watching her every move? It's a mystery to this reporter—and to half the town! And the way Ry has been glaring at Beldon... Is that merely friendly concern for Carrie? Or could it be something more like jealousy? Even the folks at the Texas Cattleman's Club seem to be holding their breath on this one....

One

"If you call me cute one more time, I swear I'm going to break every bone in your foot."

Ryan Evans lifted a considering brow and gauged the scowl on Carrie Whelan's face across the booth where they sat in the Royal Diner. She meant business. She wasn't just scowling; she was close to breathing fire as hot as the straight, shining length of silky red hair brushing small shoulders stiffened in a pique of anger.

Carrie was way too much fun to tease. Always had been. And hell, at fourteen, she *had* been cute. At twenty-four, however, it was obvious the idea that he—or any man—would regard her that way, rankled.

Sheer orneriness prompted him to push another hot button. But safety first. He cleared his throat, pulled himself up straighter and very deliberately drew his long legs back under the faded red plastic booth seat so the simmering Ms. Whelan couldn't stomp the three-inch stiletto heel of her designer boots into his instep.

"That time of the month again, is it, sweetie?" he asked with the sage and patronizing compassion of a wise and understanding man.

When she growled, he blinked, all innocence and mystified male guile. "What? What'd I say?"

She tilted her head to the side and studied him as if he were a wad of gum she'd like to scrape off the bottom of her boot. "You know, for a man of such reputed and vast experience with women, you know exactly the wrong things to say to impress a lady."

He couldn't help it. He gave it up and grinned. "Oh, so you're a lady now, are you?"

It wasn't all that long ago that little Carrie Whelan—*cute* little Carrie Whelan, his best friend, Travis Whelan's, kid sister—had declared to anyone within earshot that she was gonna be a cowboy and she'd have to be dead before anyone would catch her in anything but denim and her cowboy hat and boots.

Well, he could testify for a fact that she was still alive—very much alive—even though she'd traded denim for silk and her worn Ropers for butter-soft Italian ankle boots a few years ago. She also wore a different kind of hat these days—several different kinds, actually. Thanks to the trust fund Trav had set up for her, she didn't have to work, but the darling of Royal, Texas, society was always involved in something. If she wasn't volunteering at the Royalty Hospital burn unit or at the library, she devoted many hours a week at a tax-supported day-care center—and all that was in between organizing fund-raisers and squeezing moldy money from kindhearted old and not-so-old men with deep pockets, who were sympathetic to her causes and suckers for her smile.

And yes. She was definitely alive, Ry thought again before he could curb a quick, appreciative glance at the full, healthy breasts pushing against the ivory silk of her blouse.

But he wasn't supposed to notice that. He wasn't supposed to notice anything remotely sexy or female about Carrie.

He tugged his hat brim lower over his brow. The problem was, she was right about one thing. She wasn't cute anymore. She was beautiful...supermodel gorgeous, in fact, with those snapping hazel eyes, her tall, willow-slim body and a mouth that made a man wonder what it would feel like pressed against his bare skin.

Not him, of course. He didn't think of her that way. At least, he tried like hell not to.

Frowning, he schooled his gaze to her face again—to those mossy-green eyes—and forced a mandatory return back to surrogate-brother role. "What's got your tail in a twist, Carrie-bear?"

The look she threw him could have peeled paint off the bumper of his black four-by-four Ranger. "You're worse than my brother," she sputtered, and tipped her coffee—muddy tan and loaded with cream and sugar—to her lips. "Neither one of you takes me seriously."

Ry slumped back in the booth, resisting the urge to own up to exactly how seriously he *did* take her. How he'd seriously *like* to take her and how she could seriously mess up his head if he didn't herd his thoughts back in the right direction.

"What'd Trav do now?" he asked instead.

"What does he always do? He treats me like a child."

"He loves you," Ry said softly, and watched some of the starch ease out of her stiff spine.

She turned those hazel eyes on him. They made him think of wispy, glittering smoke. Like a night fire, embers banked but smoldering.

"What are we doing here?" she asked abruptly and with such earnest inquiry, he sobered.

"Well, the way I remember it," he said carefully, because he didn't want her getting wise to the fact that at Trav's request, Ry had been sticking pretty close to her for the past week or so, "I called to see how you were doing, you said you'd had a long day, wanted to unwind and asked me to meet you here for a cup of coffee."

She was already shaking her head. "No, I don't mean, what are we doing here, at the Royal Diner. I mean, what are *we* doing here—you and me? Look at us. It's Saturday night, for Pete's sake. Why aren't we out on the town with our respective dates, drinking champagne—or in your case, your beer of choice," she added with a smarty-pants smile, "and looking forward to a night of hot, passionate se—"

"Hold it right there." He sat up straight, pushing a hand into the space between them.

When she actually shut up, he wiped that same hand over his jaw, then resettled his hat. This was territory he had no intention of invading. "I don't think I want to be discussing my love life with you."

"Not to mention, you don't want to discuss *my* love life."

Yeah, he thought grimly, that, too. Keeping a protective eye on her in the wake of the danger that Trav's fiancée, Natalie Perez, still faced was the extent of his involvement with Carrie. He still couldn't believe he'd agreed to play watchdog slash bodyguard. Just like he couldn't believe they were having this conversation.

"I didn't hear that," he said firmly. "I didn't hear anything about you even having a love life. Because if I did, I'd have to share the info with your brother and then he'd probably feel obligated to kill the messenger—that would be *me*—before he came looking for you. And Lord have mercy on the man who messed with Travis Whelan's little sister."

She shook her head, pushed out a humorless laugh, then stared past him out the grease-and-smoke-coated window of the diner. "You can breathe easy, big guy. There's not much chance of him killing anyone anytime soon. Why? you ask. Because I don't *have* a love life, that's why. And *that's* what's got my *tail in a twist.*"

Ryan felt a small bead of sweat form on his forehead, beneath his hatband. This conversation was fast getting out of hand. "I don't think I want to hear about this, either."

Oblivious to the squirming he was doing, she met his eyes with such solemn entreaty that he couldn't look away. "Do you have any idea…do you have even a *remote* idea," she repeated for emphasis, "what it's like being twenty-four years old and still a virgin?"

Virgin? Oh, Lord.

"Why don't you say that a little louder?" he ground out, falling back on irritation to cover the instant and forbidden surge of arousal her revelation prompted. "I don't think Manny Hernandez, back in the kitchen, heard you."

She sat back with a huff of disgust. "*Manny* would probably like to give me a tumble."

He snorted. "Manny would like to give anything in skirts a tumble." Manny Hernandez, the Royal Diner's part-time cook, part-time bodybuilder was not only an outrageous flirt but also a notorious womanizer. "And what kind of way is that for a nice girl to be talking, anyway?"

"Aha!" She pointed an accusing finger, a woman

vilified. "See? *That's* the problem. Maybe I'm *not* a nice girl. Maybe I'm this red-hot sex pistol who will drive men wild with my sexual mystique and my sultry, seductive—"

"No." He cut her off again with a shake of his head. "Oh, no-ho-ho. I am *not* hearin' this."

"What's the matter, Ry? Am I getting *you* a little hot and bothered?"

Yeah. He was hot all right and wishing he'd never started teasing her in the first place. She was the one who was supposed to be squirming, not him.

"I'm about bothered enough to turn you over my knee and whoop the daylights out of your backside," he warned her in an attempt to regain his equilibrium.

Her eyes narrowed in a flirty, bad-girl grin just before she touched the tip of her tongue to the sweet, lush curve of her upper lip. "Ooo, sounds…kinky."

His heart thumped him a good one in the chest. "Carrie, I'm warning you. You keep this up and I'll—"

"You'll what? Tattle to my brother? Take me home and tie me to my bed? Which, by the way, has a fairly intriguing ring to it," she continued, her voice rising again.

He implored her with his eyes to tone it down before the handful of other diner patrons heard her— all the while fighting a vivid mental image of her naked and spread-eagle on his bed, her wrists bound to the brass headboard with silk scarves.

"Come on," he growled, feeling closed in and

steamed up and as rattled as a long-tailed cat in a room full of rocking chairs. "We're leaving."

"Leaving? Oh, I don't think so."

Looking furious and, on a more disturbing note, a little hurt, her gaze tracked around the diner before landing on and holding on to the booth in the corner. Her eyes turned feline and determined as she dug into her purse.

"You go on, Ry, but I'm staying right here and introducing myself to the new man in town. Maybe he'll see me for something other than Travis Whelan's little sister and not run for his life in the other direction."

The glare Ry shot her was wasted. She wasn't sparing even a nickel's worth of attention his way. Her eyes were still locked on a spot in the corner of the diner when she pulled out a tube of lipstick and, without consulting a mirror, expertly applied a cherry-red gloss to her lips.

Ry was still staring at her mouth, indulging in a forbidden fantasy about those lips leaving crimson tracks across his belly and about silk scarves again, when she scooted toward the edge of the seat and stood.

Finally he snapped out of it and found the presence of mind to key in to her statement—*introducing myself to the new man in town*—and followed the direction of her gaze.

He recognized the man in the corner booth. He'd never met the new doctor who had just come on board at the Royalty Hospital, but he'd seen him around. In fact, Dr. Nathan Beldon was the reason Travis specifically requested Ry keep an eye on Carrie.

"I can't put my finger on it," Trav had said with a thoughtful frown when he'd first approached Ry, "but there is something about that guy that just doesn't feel right…he's a little too slick and way too smarmy for my taste. But for some reason Carrie seems to have her sights set on meeting him."

Well, Ry thought grimly, he and Trav were of the same mind on that count. Beldon did look smarmy. The idea of Carrie taking up with him didn't sit right with him, either. It sat so wrong, in fact, that when she took a step in Beldon's direction, Ry snagged her arm and tugged her back down onto the seat.

"Beldon?" he asked, ignoring her sputtering protest for him to let go of her wrist while trying to convince himself that the coiling sensation in his gut wasn't an unsolicited curl of jealously. "You want to put the moves on Dr. Beldon?"

She stilled, shot him a considering look, then smiled. It was not a sweet smile. Neither was it innocent.

"Well, I hadn't thought of it in exactly those terms, but thanks, Ryan. Great idea. I'll 'put the moves on him,' as you so delicately put it. And if I'm lucky, by morning, maybe I won't be the last twenty-four-year-old virgin in Texas."

"Ho-kay. That does it." He knew she wasn't serious but he could see she was feeling just reckless enough to start something with the doctor she might not be able to finish. And like it or not, he was seeing enough green to know he could easily do something really stupid if this went any further. "You're going home. You are just not thinking straight tonight."

He dug into his pocket and tossed some bills on the table to cover their tab and a generous tip for Sheila, their waitress. With a steely grip on her elbow, he hustled her toward the door. Ignoring her outraged squawks of protest, he snagged her red cashmere jacket from the coatrack on the way by and shoved it into her arms.

The little gold bell hanging over the entrance door tinkled as it closed behind them. The fuming Ms. Whelan was still calling Ry names when, with his hand clamped firmly on her nape, he escorted her to her car.

"Go home," he ordered, opening the driver's-side door.

"Go to hell!" she snapped with a venomous glare.

He guided her gently but firmly behind the wheel. "Yeah, well, there's always that possibility. In the meantime, I'll just follow you to make sure you find your way."

"Neanderthal throwback," she fumed, and jerked the door shut with a slam.

"Un-huh." He leaned down, peered in the window at her fiery red cheeks and tapped his palm on the roof of her car. "No breaking the speed limit, now."

She stared straight ahead, shifted into gear and laid rubber for a full block.

Ry let out a long breath and thumbed back his Stetson. Then he walked to his sleek black truck and settled behind the wheel.

"Handled that well, didn't you, chump?" he muttered as he pulled into traffic and put pedal to metal to catch up with her.

Tomorrow he was going to have a talk with Travis. His friend could damn well find someone else to play watchdog to his sister. A eunuch maybe—which he definitely was not. And whoa…did she ever remind him of that fact. Carrie Whelan lit him up like a stick of dynamite sizzling along with a dangerously short fuse. She was a very hot, very spicy, very—did he mention *hot?*—female who he was supposed to regard as a little sister.

Damn.

He expelled a thick breath. She was *not* his sister, even though his mom and dad had taken her and Trav in when their parents had been killed in a car accident fourteen years ago. He still carried an image of sad, lost little ten-year-old Carrie crying in his arms. And it still broke his heart when he thought of what she'd suffered. But too often lately he was having a hard time dredging up the gumption to think of her as either that sweet, lost little kid or a surrogate sister.

It had been one thing when she'd been ten and he'd been eighteen. He'd even been on track when he'd reached his early twenties and she was a blossoming sixteen with a mad crush on him. He'd been sensitive to her infatuation and hadn't minded keeping an eye out for her then—at least, he hadn't when he was around Royal, which, given college and then his five-year stint on the PRCA rodeo circuit, wasn't often.

But now…well, now it was a different story. The eye he kept on Carrie Whelan now was far from fraternal—no matter how hard he tried.

Mouth set in a hard line, he followed her onto State Street. Trav would kill him if he so much as suspected Ry was thinking of Carrie in conjunction with beds and scarves and black lace, which, he'd already decided, she would look damn fine in or out of.

He shook the too-vivid picture out of his head and pulled up behind her. When her angry eyes fastened on his in her rearview mirror, he gave her a little, "Hey, how ya doin'" wave. With typical Carrie sass, she flipped him the friendly finger, ran a yellow light and left him sitting at the intersection waiting for the light to change.

"Damn woman," he sputtered with a slow shake of his head, but he was grinning when her taillights disappeared in a glut of traffic. "Gonna be the death of me."

Silky red hair. Lush plump lips. Full firm breasts.

Long slim legs. He shifted position and adjusted the fly on his jeans with the heel of his hand—like he had to do damn near every time he saw her lately.

He caught up with her a few blocks later. Five minutes after that he sat at the curb, motor idling and watched her storm out of her car and let herself into her house. Even mad as a hornet, she was a joy to watch move—all swaying hips and swishing silk.

"Death of me," he repeated under his breath as she slammed her front door behind her and a light flicked on inside. "But what a way to go."

With a warning to himself to back off—way off— he shifted into gear and headed for the Cattleman's Club. He needed a drink. A stiff one. And tomorrow he needed to see Trav. He needed to look him square in the eye and remember that the woman who was sparking his explicit sexual fantasies was his best friend's little sister.

Little *virgin* sister.

Blood rushed to his face…and to another part of his body it had no place going where Carrie was concerned.

Virgin. He'd suspected, but until she'd made the announcement to the world at large back at the diner, he hadn't wanted to know. He *really* hadn't wanted to know.

His heartbeat hit about 6.9 on the Richter scale at the thought of her innocence and what it would be like to be the first man to make love to her.

He scrubbed a hand over his jaw. Well, it wasn't

going to be him. It wasn't going to be *anybody* if
Trav, the quintessential overprotective nobody-
touches-my-sister-and-lives-to-tell-about-it   brother,
had his way. Ry knew Trav's reaction was left over
from when their parents had died. Trav had taken on
the responsibility for looking out for her with a vengeance. That had been many years ago, but he still
hadn't been able to let go. Carrie would die a spinster
if it were within Trav's power.

And what a waste that would be, Ry thought, pic-
turing the fire in her eyes and the sweet curve of her
hips as he drove through the night street.

Okay. He had to quit thinking about her that way.
And tomorrow he would. Tonight, though, he
planned to do the rest of his thinking with a drink in
his hand and let the fantasy play out. And maybe, if
he was lucky, he thought as he pulled into the Cattleman's Club parking lot, he'd have the fantasy and
her worked out of his system by morning. Maybe by
morning, he'd also figure out an excuse to give Trav
for why he couldn't be the one to keep an eye on
Carrie any longer.

Two

What are you going to do...take me home and tie me to my bed?

Good Lord, Carrie thought as she stepped out of the shower and snagged a fluffy jade-green towel from the linen closet. Had she really said that to him? To Ryan Evans, of all people?

She groaned and buried her face in the plush terry cloth. If only she'd had the good sense to stop with that. But, no. She'd had to add a really needy sounding, *Which, by the way, has a fairly intriguing ring to it,* and then hope she might actually see some spark of interest darken his eyes.

But not Ry. Oh, no. Not Carrie-bear-you've-got-your-tail-in-a-twist Evans. Interested? In her? She snorted.

"If I was a horse, maybe." Or one of those flashy four-wheel-drive vehicles—all gleaming chrome and high-gloss black enamel—he was so fond of driving.

No. Ryan Evans had never been interested in anything to do with her and a bed, unless it was trying to talk her into making his because he'd been too busy breaking broncs and chasing the town girls to make his bed himself.

She rubbed the towel through her hair and regarded her reflection in the mirror with disgust. "Some lessons are just harder than others to learn, huh, Carrie-*bear?*" she grumbled aloud and felt the anger drain as fatigue and melancholy took over.

Yeah. Some lessons were harder than others. Ry was one of the hardest.

With a sniff and a sigh, she finished drying herself off then slathered on some new lotion that smelled of sage and citrus and something softly sensual and essentially feminine. She'd actually bought it with him in mind. She snorted again. She was pathetic. What *didn't* she do without Ry in mind?

She faced her sorry self in the mirror. "So, for once and for all, what are you going to do about him?"

She honestly didn't know. She'd loved him forever. Idolized him, in fact, and he'd never seen her as anything but a kid sister. After tonight, though, since he hadn't pounced, panted or even tiptoed around any of the not-so-subtle invitations she'd lobbed his way, it was pretty clear that he never would see her any other way.

She bit her lower lip thoughtfully and faced the unalterable truth. "Maybe it's time to give it up."

She drew in a deep breath, let it out as the thought settled like lead. Yeah. Maybe it was time.

Slipping into a clean, oversize nightshirt that still smelled fresh from the dryer, then tugging a pair of socks over her cold tootsies, she wandered into the living room working a brush through her wet hair as she went. Snagging the remote on the way by the end table, she punched it toward the TV then plunked down on the sofa. The soft navy-blue chenille throw felt snuggly and warm as she dragged it from the back of the sofa and settled it over her upraised knees. It would have felt infinitely better if she'd been snuggled up to Ry.

She caught herself. "You're doing it again, Whelan. It's not going to happen. Not with Ry, so just give it up."

For the next five minutes she tried to get used to the idea that she did need to do just that. She needed to once and for all let go of the fantasy of him and her together.

So she thought about her volunteer work at the burn center, of the kids at day care. Anything to take her mind off him as she channel surfed, punching the remote with one hand and unconsciously fiddling with the hair on the left side of her forehead where the cowlick she always fought to tame remained as stubborn as ever.

"Nothing. You'd think you could find one thing among the dozens of cable channels that looks interesting," she sputtered aloud. One thing to distract her or to snag her thoughts away from the lost cause that was Ry Evans.

Disgusted with herself, she flicked off the TV and tossed the remote on the coffee table. The photo album on the second shelf caught and held her attention. She stared at it for a long time before finally giving in to the temptation to take a little stroll down memory lane.

A picture of her mom and dad and her and Trav brought a bittersweet smile. She trailed her index finger across the smiling faces of her parents. She'd been nine; Trav was seventeen when the photo had been taken. They'd been in Fort Worth at the stock show. It was one of the last photos taken of them all together before the accident that had claimed Sue and Joe Whelan's young lives.

She wished with everything in her that it wasn't so difficult to attach animation to the still photos. She'd always wanted to remember them as three-dimensional and full of life...but after fourteen years, those vital connections had faded along with the picture's color.

She'd gotten on with her life a long time ago. The pain had ebbed to something tolerable. A misty sort of longing had replaced the cruel, agonizing grief that had shattered the sanctity of her perfect little world. But all these years later, she still missed them.

With one last, lingering look, she turned the page...and there he was. Ryan. Lanky and lean, broad-shouldered and brown-eyed. He'd been eighteen to her ten, larger than life, grinning and strong. Her heart tripped, like it always did when she saw him, when she thought of him, when she let herself believe he could be more to her than a surrogate big brother after his parents had taken her in following the accident that had left her bewildered and withdrawn and confused.

To make matters worse, Travis had signed up for the U.S. Marines just before the accident and had had to leave shortly after. She'd never felt so alone. Even now her eyes stung as she remembered more than one lost, lonely night when Ry would find her in the room his mother had decorated with such special attention to please the sad little person she had been.

He'd stand broad-shouldered and thoughtful in her doorway, a pained, helpless expression momentarily crossing his handsome face. Then he'd smile and charge into her room like a big, noisy teddy bear and proceed to tease a grin out of her, coax her into a giggle and, ultimately and unintentionally, stir the woman budding inside her ten-year-old soul into loving him.

"We're your family now," Ry's mom had told her more than once after that horrible day. "You and Travis belong to us. Your daddy was our foreman. I loved your mother like a sister and your father was like a brother to my John...just like Travis and Ryan are like brothers. Just like you are our daughter now.''

Very quietly Carrie closed the album and hugged it to her breast, as Sandy used to hug her to hers. This album represented her past. So did the lifelong fantasy of Ryan falling in love with her. Tonight had finally made her accept that it wasn't meant to be.

Ryan Evans was *not* her Mr. Right.

''So...this is it, then, isn't it?'' she whispered aloud, and felt her heartbeat flutter with sadness. ''The infamous defining moment.''

A tear trickled down her cheek at the reality that she'd finally decided to let it go. It was time to move on. She wanted a relationship. She wanted a husband and little chubby-cheeked kids. And since she'd finally accepted Ry wasn't going to be a part of that picture, she was determined to find someone who would be. Soon.

A knock sounded at her door, startling her. She rose, sniffed and—brushing the moisture from her cheeks—walked to her foyer, checking the clock on the way. It was almost midnight. A quick look through the peephole had her heart jumping again.

She threw open the door. ''Ryan.''

''Hey, bear,'' he said, with a lopsided grin. ''Can I come in...just for a second...or did I officially make myself persona non gratis in your book tonight?''

She looked at his beautiful, lived-in face, at the smiling brown eyes that made her think of blended whiskey or pricey bourbon and had warmed her like a bonfire more times than she cared to remember. A fine, hook-shaped scar rode the ridge of his cheekbone beneath his left eye—a reminder of his rodeo days and a run-in with a bronc that had all but stomped him into the arena floor.

There were other scars. His hands were peppered with the little nicks and scrapes of a working cattleman. The little bump on the bridge of his nose signified it had been broken once…probably by a horse, possibly in a bar fight. She knew he'd had his share of them, too, when he was rodeoing. The road, she knew, had been rough, and fists had sometimes flown as freely as the BS and the dreams of an NFR championship.

He'd come close to catching his dream. So close.

And so had she. She'd come close to reaching her dream of being loved by him. At least she'd come close in her mind.

"Carrie? Hellloooo? Where'd you go, sweet pea?"

She blinked, realized she'd gone back there…to that place where he filled her senses and her thoughts and kept her from moving away from him and toward her future.

"Sorry," she said, and opened the door wider so

he could step inside out of the chill. "You... surprised me," she said lamely. "What's up?"

He lifted a broad shoulder, gave her a sheepish look. "Just wanted to make sure we were okay after...you know."

She tilted her head. "After you herded me out of the diner like a maverick calf?"

He actually flinched, then grinned. "Ah...yeah. After that."

"Don't sweat it," she said, determined to turn over this new leaf and ignore the slow, melting action going on around her heart. "But don't let it happen again, okay?"

He considered her as he stood just inside her foyer. "Does that mean you're still planning on—"

"Putting the *moves* on Dr. Beldon?" she interrupted cheekily, then told him how it was going to be. "Know what, Ry? I think you and Trav—and for that matter, the rest of the guys at the Cattleman's Club—all function on some misguided notion that every female in the free world needs saving."

He looked a little stunned.

"What? You don't think I know what goes on behind closed doors at that place? Trav is my brother, for Pete's sake. He disappears...sometimes for days. For that matter, so do you and the others. And isn't it coincidental that shortly after you all pop up again, world or local headlines report on some heinous crime being thwarted, or some country being saved from a disastrous coup by some radical extremist group?''

She laughed at the pained and panicked expression on his face.

''Oh, don't look so shell-shocked, Ry. Your secrets are safe. Case in point, Natalie. I know something's up with her and the baby. And I know you guys are knee-deep in it, trying to bring down whatever chased her to Texas. I hope you succeed. I love her like a sister, and little Autumn...well, she owns me heart and soul. I want them safe. I want that hunted look erased from Natalie's eyes.''

''Carrie...'' He said her name with such a preemptive wariness, she actually took pity on him.

''Yeah, okay, fine. You guys don't really save nations or damsels in distress. You aren't secretly investigating the horrible things that happened to Natalie. I got it. It's your story, you can tell it any way you want to. But if you *were*...I know you would get to the bottom of it.

''In the meantime—'' she held up a hand when he would have cut her off ''—I don't have anything to do with Natalie's dilemma...which means I don't need protection. And since I don't, what I do and who I do it with is really none of your business.''

It could have been, she thought with more than a pinch of regret. But it's not and you're the one who wants it that way.

Something had replaced the shock in his expression. He looked a little sad...there might even have been a little regret in his eyes. It didn't matter. She could no longer afford to care. But damn him, the next words out of his mouth made her want to.

"You will always be my business, sweetie." He touched a hand to her cheek, and then, as if realizing what he'd done, let it fall. "Just…just be careful, okay?"

Then he reached out again, as if he couldn't help himself, and cupped her nape with his broad hand. He drew her toward him, smelling of leather and sage and a little of horses when he leaned down and pressed his lips against her forehead. "'Night, Carrie-bear. Lock up behind me."

She was still standing there, rooted to the spot, her heart making one final, futile dive when his truck's engine fired and he drove away.

"Goodbye, Ryan," she whispered to the empty street, knowing she was finally saying goodbye to the hope she'd fostered for fourteen years.

She went to bed a little while later, pushing Ryan further and further out of her mind, more determined than ever to get on with her life. But who was she going to get on with her life with?

"And wasn't *that* an interesting sentence?" she asked herself aloud with a roll of her eyes.

Speaking of eye rolling… She ran through a list of likely candidates for the position of Mr. Right. It was a very short list. And with good reason. Travis grilled every prospective boyfriend until they were as charred as a well-done T-bone.

Oh, she knew her brother meant well. He didn't mean to send every boyfriend she'd ever had running for their lives rather than toughing it out and actually taking a stab at a relationship with her—but he did. Aside from Ryan, Trav was the main reason she was still single and resenting the fact that she was a ripe twenty-four and still a virgin.

"Well, you've taken the protector role too seriously for too long, brother mine," she murmured as she rolled over, punched her pillow and snuggled deeper into the covers. She was no longer the ten-year-old little girl, lost and confused and missing her mom and dad. She was a woman now—at least in years. In experience, however, she was as green as meadow grass.

But not for much longer. Tonight had really, truly, once and for all cinched it. She was ready to make the transition to wild oats. Since Ry was not going to be the man to guide her around that exciting corner, she was just going to have to find someone else who would.

There had to be *someone* who wasn't intimidated by her brother. Someone who hadn't grown up around here wouldn't know enough to be afraid of Travis. Someone new in town.

Someone like Dr. Nathan Beldon.

It just kept coming back to him.

Yeah. She could settle for a doctor.

Settle.

She pulled in a deep breath, let it out. It probably

didn't say much about her strength of character that she was considering settling for any man who didn't run from Travis. It also pretty much told the tale that she wasn't evolved, in the feminist sense.

"Not everyone is cut out to be a mover and a shaker or a corporate ball breaker," she muttered, and flipped over onto her back again. "No crime in that."

She made a difference in her own way. She liked her volunteer work at the library with her friend Stephanie Firth, and her work at the burn clinic. She also loved organizing fund-raisers. But what she really enjoyed was the time she spent at the day-care center.

She loved kids. Short ones, shy ones, snotty-nosed ones, even the ones that bit. And she wanted kids of her own—with the man she wanted to spend the rest of her life with. Or at least with a man who was willing to spend his life with her.

And then, of course, there was that other little thing. That virgin thing. She was so tired of celibacy. She wanted to know what all the fuss was about. If Nathan Beldon ended up being the one to show her, maybe he could also be the one she could potentially start a life and raise her babies with.

And to hell with what Trav or Ryan said.

"I thought we had this settled, bud." Trav Whelan clasped a hand on Ry's shoulder the next afternoon as they cozied up to the bar in the Cattleman's Club.

His expression was filled with stymied disappointment. "Don't back out on me now."

Ry grimaced and scratched his ear. And came up blank. This conversation was not going the way he'd planned it. He'd had his arguments lined up like spit-and-polished soldiers. Put one of the other guys— *any* of the other guys involved with the situation— in charge of looking out for Carrie until this mystery surrounding Natalie Perez and her baby was solved. Ry was a lover, not a fighter, right? Yeah…he'd been in on some of the covert missions the Cattleman's Club members sometimes found themselves diving into feet first for the greater good, but there were much better men for this particular job.

Trav, however, didn't see it that way and didn't plan on taking no for an answer. And he was doing a damn fine job of guilting Ry into forgetting all the valid reasons why it was a bad idea for him to be the one to ride herd on Carrie.

"You are my *man*," Trav continued with a come-on, step-up-to-the-plate smile. "You have *always* been my man. Hell, Ry, you've been around long enough to know I can't take a chance on some opportunistic SOB who might try to take advantage of her. You're the only one I can turn to…and *I* can't keep an eye on her. Not until this is over."

Torn between the need to wrangle a way out of certain disaster and his loyalty to Trav, Ry let out a long sigh while Trav settled in to draw a little more blood.

"I'm a daddy. A *daddy*," Trav repeated as if he still couldn't believe his good fortune, "and the lady in my life... Ry, you know both Natalie and the baby are still at risk."

Yeah, Ryan knew. So, evidently, did Carrie. He was still chewing on that little bit of news. He was still a little staggered by her conjectures. She'd been dead-on right. About a lot of things. The Texas Cattleman's Club did get involved in covert missions. It was part of their code of honor and their mission. Justice, peace, leadership...what they did was always for the greater good.

Most recently, several Club members—Trav and himself along with David Sorenson, Clint Andover, Alex Kent and Sheik Darin ibn Shakir—had been trying to unravel the mystery that started one chilly night in November and just kept getting more bizarre. Yes, they knew a lot more now than they had that night when the then-unidentified woman had stumbled into the Royal Diner with a newborn baby girl and a cool half a million dollars stuffed in a diaper bag, but there were still questions.

That woman, who had promptly collapsed, fallen into a coma and only recently recovered and regained her memory, was Natalie Perez, now Travis's fiancée. The baby was Trav's baby, the unexpected but wonderful result of an affair they had both decided it was best to walk away from almost a year ago.

The two men became very quiet. Ry pondered the label on the long-neck he cupped loosely in his hands on the bar in front of him. "How is Natalie?" he asked finally. "And little Autumn?"

Trav contemplated his own beer, as sober as Ry had ever seen him. "They're doing okay. Man...I can't believe I ever walked away from her. I can't believe I almost lost them. That bastard Birkenfeld...he could have killed Natalie, sold our baby."

Ry let out a deep breath, the enormity of the situation weighing heavily on his shoulders as he recalled the details. He hadn't been at the diner that November night when Natalie showed up with a Texas Cattleman's Club business card clutched in her hand. Neither had Travis or Darin, who had both been out of the country on assignment until the end of the December.

Maybe if Trav had been in town when Natalie had first appeared on the scene, they'd be further ahead of the game. But he hadn't, and it was only when she'd spotted Travis at the New Year's Eve party after he'd returned to Royal from Europe and a TCC mission, that Natalie had started to remember.

She'd finally recalled Travis and their brief but intense affair that had resulted in little Autumn. It wasn't until weeks later that she'd remembered why she'd ended up in Royal carrying all that money in a diaper bag. The story was so bizarre that even now Ry had trouble digesting the magnitude and the far-reaching effects.

Natalie had been worked at a birthing clinic run by Dr. Roman Birkenfeld. Over several months she'd noticed that an alarming number of single women had lost their babies at birth. She'd been so alarmed she'd decided to secretly search the computer files. When she did, she discovered that the babies hadn't really died but had been sold. Before she could confront Dr. Birkenfeld or go to the police with this damning information, she'd gone into labor.

And that's when her trouble had begun. The good doctor, it seemed, had had the same plans for Natalie's baby as he'd had for the others. He'd drugged her, and the next morning, after she'd given birth, she'd realized he intended to tell her, as he had the other women, that her baby had died. Somehow Natalie had escaped the clinic undetected, and followed Dr. Birkenfeld and his nurse accomplice to the airport where Natalie was positive they intended to fly with the baby to the prospective buyers.

When the nurse took the baby into a rest room to change her diaper, Natalie had made her move. She shoved the woman to the floor, grabbed the baby and the diaper bag—which, it turned out, was full of money that the TCC men now held in the club's safe. She'd fled to the bus station, but Birkenfeld and his nurse had caught up with her in Amarillo.

And from that point on, Natalie's memory was still a blank slate, which was why Trav and the rest of the guys were still on guard.

Ry angled Trav a look. "Has she remembered anything else?" he asked, knowing they needed something more to help them resolve this nasty business.

Travis shook his head. "No. Everything after Amarillo is pretty fuzzy. All she remembers of Birkenfeld catching up with her is that there was a struggle and she hit her head." He stopped, and Ry could see a hundred emotions cloud his friend's face. Everything from rage to helplessness to relief that his woman and his child were safe to frustration that Birkenfeld had dropped out of sight but was still a threat. They wanted to put this entire episode to bed.

"She doesn't know how she got away from them," Trav continued. "Last night she told me that the only thing that kept her going was knowing she had to stay conscious long enough to find me."

He swallowed hard. "And then I wasn't there for her."

"Hey." Ry's hand on Trav's shoulder pulled him out of his anguish to meet Ry's eyes. "You're here for her now. You're here for both of them."

All the TCC guys were, until they caught Birkenfeld and his nurse, who were still on the loose and evidently desperate, if the threats against Natalie's life were any indication. Ry figured they were. And after Tara Roberts, who had taken Natalie home with her to recuperate, had ended up with her house mysteriously burning down, none of the TCC men felt they could let down their guards or ease up on their continuing investigation.

"Birkenfeld is still out there somewhere," Travis

said, his voice chillingly cold. "Until he's caught and put behind bars, neither Natalie nor Autumn are safe." He turned to Ry. "That's why I need you, man. Carrie—"

"Is a big girl," Ry insisted, still determined to work his way out of this. He was more or less in agreement with Carrie on this issue. "I really don't know why you think she needs protection. She's not a part of this."

"But *I* am. And I figure Birkenfeld knows that. Do you feel comfortable—no, strike *comfortable*. Do you feel one hundred percent *sure* that this sick bastard who drugs women and tells them their babies are dead so he can sell them, wouldn't stoop so low as to try to get to Natalie through me and what's mine?"

Ry closed his eyes, knowing in his heart of hearts that Trav was right. Ry didn't feel one hundred percent sure about that. And since Carrie was part of Trav's world, he had a legitimate point. "You're right. It takes a twisted as well as a corrupt mind to do what he's done."

"And it takes someone I trust to look out for my sister until we find him and finish this."

Ry rocked his beer bottle slowly back and forth on the bar and finally nodded in defeat. How could he turn Trav down in the face of such a compelling argument?

He expelled another deep breath. "Yeah. Okay.

Okay. I'll do it. But I still don't understand what Nathan Beldon has to do with any of this.''

Trav shrugged. "Probably nothing.''

Ry whipped his head toward his friend. "Then *why* am I watching out for him?''

"Because I don't like him.'' Trav gave Ry a bland look. "Do I have to have another reason?''

Three

―――

"**I** don't believe I'm doing this," Ryan muttered under his breath later that night. He tugged his Resistol low over his brow. Slumped behind the wheel of his new black SUV, he watched with a scowl as Carrie walked toward the Royal Diner on Nathan Beldon's arm.

She worked fast. He'd give her that. Or maybe it was Beldon who'd "put the moves" on her. Now, there was a statement that was going to haunt him into the next decade. Just like spying on Carrie was going to be his undoing.

Trav may call it keeping an eye on her, but Ry figured Wayne Vincente, the Royal police chief might have a different take on it—like maybe *stalk-*

ing. And Ry, hell, he called it a whole lot of other things. Like *uncomfortable,* and *stupid* and…hey. He sat up straight, all senses on red alert. Had he seen that right? Had the slimeball doctor's hand slipped a gentleman's distance too low at the small of Carrie's back where he'd planted it with a little too much familiarity?

The diner door closed behind them before he had a chance to decide if it had been an accident or an illusion.

Slimeball.

Ry didn't even know the guy, yet after seeing that—whatever *that* was—the assessment felt like a good fit. Without an ounce of hesitation, he slipped out of his SUV and headed for the diner. Trav wanted him to watch out for Carrie, so that's what he was going to do. And that's what this was about. A favor for a friend. Nothing more. He'd made up his mind last night that no matter what he wanted or how hot she was, Carrie was as off-limits romantically as a top secret military intelligence project.

And with that thought fueling him, he opened the Royal Diner door and prepared to run a little creative interference.

Nathan Beldon really was quite attractive, in a reserved, sophisticated sort of way, Carrie decided as she settled in across the booth from him.

"You sure this is all right?" the good doctor asked with a smile that was apologetic and attentive and...interested, she realized with pleased surprise. Interested in a way that Ry had never been.

She pushed thoughts of Ry from her mind and smiled back.

"This is fine," she assured him. And it was more than fine that he actually looked a little shy... uncertain, even.

Imagine. A man who looked like him, as imposing and as self-confident as him, feeling uncertain of her. Why, it just set her little Southern heart all aflutter.

She smiled at herself and her silliness all the while covertly assessing her impromptu dinner partner. She'd been leaving her volunteer shift at the hospital when she'd run into him in the parking lot, introduced herself and asked him if he'd like to join her for dinner.

She'd been pretty proud of herself. She'd been cool, confident, not overly friendly...and he'd very graciously accepted her offer. Eagerly accepted her offer, even.

And now here they were. She shot a covert glance at him over the top of her menu. Nathan Beldon wasn't what you'd call blatantly handsome—not like Travis or Ryan with their in-your-face, drop-dead-gorgeous good looks. His was more of a classic, polished appeal. His brown eyes weren't flirty and warm like theirs; his were far more serious. Not that that was a bad thing, just different from what she was used to.

He was also very tall. Ryan was tall—an even six

feet—but Nathan was perhaps a couple of inches taller. She liked that, she decided. At five-nine, she liked to sometimes feel a little delicate, liked to look up into a pair of interested eyes. And Nathan's dark eyes were definitely showing some interest.

He wasn't built like Ry, either. While Ry was all muscle and sinew and athletic grace, Nathan Beldon was on the slim side and moved with a refined elegance that made her wonder what it would be like to dance with him. Could she be Ginger to his Fred?

Could it be she'd been watching too many old, classic movies? Again she grinned at herself and all these sappy romantic notions.

"Next time," Nathan said, his cultured voice so softly hopeful it dragged her away from her musings, "we'll go to Claire's...or am I assuming too much?"

She smiled, pleased. "No...you're not assuming too much at all. I'd...like that very much."

She also very much liked the way his perfectly styled hair—so dark brown it was almost black—completed the tall dark and handsome look, even if his hair was a little finer, a little thinner than Ry's, which was a thick, lush sable and always looked as if he'd just run his hands through it in frustration.

"As a matter of fact," she added, catching and hating herself for comparing Nathan to Ryan for about the hundredth time since she'd run into Nathan at the hospital earlier, "Claire's is one of my favorite spots."

Royal's quaint and classy French restaurant was

noted for its romantic ambiance and excellent wines. An invitation to Claire's came with a wealth of implied possibilities.

"Then we definitely have something else to look forward to," Nathan said with another one of those smiles that promised more than a casual cup of coffee after a romantic evening.

"Yes," she said, determined to focus on him and the attention he was giving her and banish Ryan from her mind, "we definitely do."

"Hey, folks."

Carrie smiled up at Sheila who appeared with a carafe of coffee and her order pad. "Hey, Sheila."

"What would you like?" Nathan asked without acknowledging the waitress.

Sheila was one of Carrie's favorite people in the whole world. The bubble-gum-blowing, forty-something waitress was blousy and blatantly sexual in her too-tight uniform and bold makeup. She was also forthright and funny and her cat-and-mouse come-ons to Manny, who flirted and teased with everyone but who, Carrie suspected, secretly had it bad for Sheila, cracked her up.

"Have you met Sheila?" Carrie interjected, deciding Nathan hadn't actually meant to be impolite, but instead was simply feeling the weight of "new person in town" syndrome and still felt a little uncomfortable with the locals. "She's an institution at the Royal Diner."

"Sweetie, I'm an institution in Texas," Sheila informed her with her best Mae West moue. "How you doin', Doc?" she added as Nathan slowly lifted his gaze from the menu.

"A…pleasure, I'm sure," he managed, looking uncomfortable even as he forced a smile that Carrie strongly suspected was for her benefit.

Determined to be generous and assume his actions were shy, not snobbish, Carrie folded her menu and smiled up at Sheila. "I'll have the soup. And a small salad."

"Ranch on the side, right?"

"You got it."

"And for you, Doc?" Sheila asked.

His shoulders stiffened slightly then relaxed. As Carrie watched, wondering if perhaps he was a little snobbish after all, he folded his menu, looked at Sheila and manufactured a smile. "I'll try the sirloin. Medium rare."

"Comes with a baked spud and a side of 'slaw."

"Fine," he said and, dismissing her, redirected his gaze at Carrie.

She'd just decided she'd imagined Nathan's discomfort when the last voice in the entire free world that she wanted to hear boomed into the confined space she'd carved out for her and Nathan.

"Fine with me, too, sweet cheeks. I'll have what he's having."

Carrie froze at the sound of Ryan Evan's voice.

With a barely suppressed groan, she looked up to see him standing there—all-American good looks, all-Texas brass, all rough-hewn charisma geared up to charm the socks off the world in general and Sheila in particular.

His cheeks were ruddy from the chill of the wind and the cool February night. His shearling coat was open at his throat, his hat tugged low over his brow, beneath which his brown eyes danced with intelligence and a blatantly flirtatious sparkle. Every woman with a beating heart had to have felt it stall, then catch at the mouthwatering picture he made standing there…pure animal magnetism, rough-and-tumble cowboy grace.

"Hello, you handsome devil," Sheila cooed.

"You made up your mind to marry me yet?" Ry teased with a grin as he dropped a kiss on Sheila's cheek.

"Darlin'," Sheila drawled, "if I thought you could keep up with me, we'd negotiate, but I'm a realist, not a dreamer…unlike you, who can only dream of what you're missing out on."

"What a woman." Ry chuckled as Sheila walked away with their orders and, despite Carrie's death grip on the tabletop and her obvious intention to stay firmly put on the outside edge of the booth seat, he nudged her aside and squeezed onto the bench beside her.

He smelled of the chilly evening and of leather and everything familiar yet illusive, and she hated him in that moment almost as much as she'd always loved him for his unconscious ability to send her into awareness overload.

He turned his gaze first to Nathan, who, Carrie noticed from the corner of her eye, appeared to be sliding toward a slow boil over Ry's unwelcome intrusion.

"Well, now," Ryan said, all aw-shucks grin and innocent eyes as he turned to her, "isn't this nice? Never dreamed I'd find some dinner company tonight. Y'all don't mind do you?" he barreled on as if Carrie wasn't giving him the evil eye and singeing him with silent messages to "git while the gittin' was still good."

"Great," he said before she could open her mouth, and turned that good-ol'-boy grin on Nathan. "Evans. Ryan Evans." He extended his hand across the booth top. "Nelson Beldon, right?"

"Nathan. *Dr.* Nathan Beldon," Nathan corrected him stiffly, and because he'd been left with no choice, he met Ry's hand across the gray Formica.

"Doc," Ry said with a nodding smile while he exerted, in Carrie's opinion, just a little too much enthusiasm in an extended handshake that finally ended with a small grimace of pain on Nathan's face.

God, she thought on a long sigh. Did that really just happen? Did Ry just try to outmuscle Nathan? If she didn't know better, she'd think he was pulling a junkyard-dog stunt and marking his territory. Which, of course, was as ridiculous a notion as the one she'd bought into for the past fourteen years.

"What are you doing here, Ryan?" she asked through a clenched jaw and totally false smile as she fought with everything in her to ignore the way his muscled thigh felt pressed against hers. It was solid and hard and hot.

"Same thing you are, Carrie-bear. Refueling. So—" he turned his attention away from her and back to Nathan as she quietly slid out of physical contact range "—how are you finding Royal, Nolan?"

"Nathan," Carrie corrected him with a hard stare. "His name is Nathan."

Another country boy grin. "Nolan. Nathan. Sorry, pal. So…you're a vet, right?"

Carrie closed her eyes and counted to ten as fire flooded her cheeks. She was about to clarify, yet again, when Nathan handled it.

"Physician. OB/GYN, actually. And you? It would appear by your outfit that you'd be a cowboy, correct?"

Her eyes flew open. She grinned. Whoa. Score one for the doc.

Okay. Maybe score half a point, she decided, when she saw a vein bulge out on Nathan's forehead.

Beside her, though, Ry's grin just got broader, making it apparent who was still getting the best of whom.

The evening quickly went downhill from there.

"Just what, in the name of everything sane, did you think you were doing?" Carrie demanded as she watched Nathan walk out of the diner, his shoulders stiff.

Beside her, polishing off the last of his dinner, Ryan paused with his fork midair. "What are you talking about, darlin'?"

It was the last straw. She slugged him.

"Ouch." He rubbed his biceps, grimaced. "That hurt."

"It couldn't possibly have hurt enough," she groused and, crossing her arms over her breasts, slumped back in the booth seat.

He pretended to study her with a concerned frown. "Oh. Oh," he repeated, as if the bricks she'd have dearly loved to drop on his thick head had finally landed dead center. "I interrupted something, didn't I?"

She tilted her head, narrowed her eyes. "Gosh... ya *think?*"

He had the good sense to finally look guilty. So guilty that she almost felt sorry for him. Almost.

"I think I hate you."

He became quiet before setting down his fork and drawing a deep breath. "So...umm...you think this guy might be special?"

She gave a weary snort and made herself ignore the feel of his warm callused fingers as he lifted a hand to her face to tuck her hair behind her ear. "Well, I'll probably never know now, will I? Not after that dog-and-pony show you put on tonight."

She could feel his warm-brown eyes on her but refused to look at him. Finally he dropped his hand.

"Hate to break it to you, sunshine," he said, "but if he scares off that easily, he's not only *not* special, he hasn't got what it takes to breathe the same air you do."

Carrie crossed her arms on the booth tabletop, dropped her forehead to rest there and expelled an exasperated sigh. "All I wanted was dinner and a chance to get to know him. Was that too much to ask?"

Ry looked down at her riot of shiny red hair, at the weary slump of her shoulders and felt a curl of real guilt coil in his belly. He lifted a hand, let it hover over her slim back before finally giving in to the urge and letting it settle there. When she didn't object, he gently rubbed. She was so slight. The flesh and bone and delicate muscle beneath her kelly-green sweater was warm and resilient.

He only meant to soothe her and assuage a little of his guilt. Instead, as his palm skated over what was obviously the clasp of her bra, he got lost in a fantasy that filled his mind way too often lately.

Would her bra be black, he wondered. Would it match her panties? The thought of seeing her in nothing but black silk and fragile lace warmed by her skin and peeled away by his hands had him swallowing hard. And yet he couldn't make himself stop.

He could see himself tunneling his hands up and under that sweater, unfastening her bra, drawing her back against him and filling his palms with her breasts. He could imagine the heat of her, the weight, the giving softness surrounding the hard spears of her nipples pressing against his palm while his other hand slipped down across her ribs, and lower, lingering on her slim hip before his fingers skimmed past her belly, under her panties and found the silky heat of her.

The length of his erection pressed against his fly.

Again. Because of her. Trav's little sister.

He let out a heavy breath. Withdrew his hand. Gave himself a mental head slap.

"How about some pie?" he asked in a voice that barely sounded like his own.

She lifted her head, looked at him.

Her hair was slightly mussed. Her cheek had a little crease from the pressure of her face pressed against her sweater sleeve. It's what she would look like in the morning, he realized. After he'd made love to her all night. Sleepy and sated and... Whoops, the heat in her eyes was anger not passion, and burst him out of his little sensual haze like a pin pricking a balloon.

"Pie? That's how you fix what you did just now?"

In spite of himself and his guilt and his arousal, he grinned. "Used to do the trick," he said hopefully.

"Yeah. When I was twelve."

"Takes a little more than pie to make you feel good now, is that it, bear?"

The moment he said it, he regretted it. Because it conjured a dozen thoughts about ways he'd like to make her feel good. Starting with her mouth, working slowly down from there. Oh, yeah. He'd make her feel good. He'd make them both feel good.

"What it takes," she said, dragging her hair back from her face, "is a little…just a *little*…respect for my feelings."

"I respect you, sweetie. I'm just not sure Nelson does."

"Nathan," she said with fire in her eyes. "His name is Nathan, and I don't really care what you think of him, do you understand?

"Now, move," she ordered in a mercurial shift from down-and-out to down-and-dirty mad. "And for future reference," she added when he let her out of the booth, deciding he'd better make way or confront the wrath of a royally ticked-off redhead, "I don't want to see your face in my face the next time I'm faced with Nathan's face…is that clear?"

"I…um…"

"Good!"

Not good, Ry thought as he watched her storm out of the diner.

"When you gonna do something about that?" Sheila asked, sidling over to the booth and slapping his dinner check into his hand.

"Do something about what?" he asked, absently digging into his hip pocket for his wallet, his eyes still on Carrie's sweet little backside as she sashayed at a fast, hot clip out the door.

"About that case you've got on her...about the case she's got on you."

He whipped his head around. Opened his mouth. Closed it. Cleared his throat.

"Yeah...it's that obvious," Sheila said, answering his unasked question with a "you poor bumbling buffoon" shake of her head before she walked away.

It crossed his mind to deny it...but he knew he'd only be digging a deeper hole. Like a six-foot-deep hole that Trav would dump him in to bury the body if he ever found out Ry had the hots—and possibly a whole lot more—for his little sister.

"Ain't this just a fine kettle of catfish," he mumbled as he tossed some bills on the booth top and resettled his hat. The best thing he could do for himself was stay away from her, and the only thing Trav wanted him to do was ride herd.

Lust or *loyalty*. Pared down to those two words, there could only be one choice. He headed for the door and hoped he had the strength of character to choose the right one.

Damn Ryan Evans. And damn this stupid cow town. He'd been trying to figure an angle to get to Carrie Whelan for days and when he finally found the opportunity, Evans had cut him off at the knees.

Seething with rage and still smelling of that row-rent greasy-spoon diner, he let himself into the apartment he'd rented last month on the west end of Royal. He stormed straight for his bedroom, angrily tossing his keys on the top of the bureau. With jerky motions that relayed the extent of his rage over Evans's interference, he unbuttoned his shirt and yanked it out of his trousers.

"You're home early."

He whipped his head toward the bed where a very blond, very naked woman lay beneath the sheets, smiling at him.

He closed his eyes, swore. "What are you doing here?"

"Ooo. Testy tonight, are we? What's the matter, darling? Didn't your little tryst with sweet Carrie Whelan go as well as you'd planned?"

"I told you," he snapped, ignoring her sarcasm and stepping out of his pants, "we have to be careful. As far as anyone knows, you're my nurse. Nothing more. And you sure as hell shouldn't be here."

"I was careful," she said with a pout and a come-hither look that drained some of his anger and stirred his lust. "No one saw me come in. And you're glad I'm here. Admit it. For heaven's sake, don't be such a poop. It's been days since we've spent any... *quality* time together," she added with a suggestive smile. "I've missed you."

He gave her a hard stare, considered throwing her out with an admonishment to stay out until he told her it was safe, but then she peeled back the covers and opened her arms. Her body was as lush as her cheery red lips. With a toss of her head, her long mane of platinum-blond hair fell enticingly over her shoulders.

"You don't really want me to go...do you Roman?"

He let out a deep breath, crossed to the bed. "How many times have I told you not to call me by my real name?"

"All right. All right." Now it was *her* voice that was filled with impatience. Her pale blue eyes that heated to electric flame. "*Nathan.* I know the drill. You've reminded me often enough. As long as we're stuck in this dust trap, you're Dr. Nathan Beldon, not Dr. Roman Birkenfeld, and I'm nurse Mary Campbell, not Marci Carson. Now...you don't *really* want me to go, do you...Nathan?"

His gaze raked her body. No. He didn't want her to go. At least not for another hour or so. He still needed her to play out this scam. And he needed to work off some of his tension with Nurse "Goodbody."

He hadn't been thinking straight lately. He needed his wits about him. He needed to regroup and refocus and marshal his thoughts, reassess his plan. Forget about what he'd done to the real Dr. Nathan Beldon whose identity he'd stolen...quit worrying about being found out. Even if the Dallas PD found Beldon's body—and he'd made sure they wouldn't—the police wouldn't be able to pin the murder on him. He wasn't stupid. He hadn't gotten where he was by being stupid.

All he needed to do was keep it together so he could get to Natalie Perez. The bitch. She was the one who'd screwed things up. She'd gotten wise to his black-market baby ring and skipped with both her baby and his money—money he'd been hoarding from baby sales for months so he could pay off the loan sharks who'd covered his Atlantic City gambling debts. He was as good as dead if he didn't get the baby and the money back. Thanks to Natalie Perez, he'd been roughed up good and his life had been threatened—with the promise that they would not let him die easily if he didn't make good on his loan. Soon.

He swiped a damp palm over his jaw. He had to get to that baby. And he had to recover the half million she'd stolen from him so he could get the monkey off his back.

So, no. He didn't want the woman warming his bed to leave. He wanted some relief from all this pressure. Keeping up the sham of his false ID, constantly being on guard against the loan sharks catching up with him, figuring out angles to get out from under…it was taking a toll. He wasn't sleeping. He'd lost weight.

"Come on, baby," Marci purred, and lay back on the pillow. "I'll make you feel better."

Yeah, he thought. She was a regular Florence Nightingale…and he was in need of a healing hand.

He crossed over to the bed and stretched out on top of her. He'd worry about Carrie Whelan in the morning. Stupid little do-gooder. She was an easy mark—ripe for the picking. She was as naive as a baby and already halfway in love with him. She was only a means to an end—totally expendable. Everyone in this little cow town was easy to fool... including the hospital board. They hadn't even questioned the Texas medical credentials he'd lifted from Beldon's office. Stupid yokels. It had been so easy to infiltrate the medical community and gain hospital privileges. He'd simply approached the chief of staff and stated he was interested in participating in their physician's exchange program. The administrator, who just happened to have been looking for a replacement for a doctor who had recently moved out of state, had been happy as a damn clam to take him on.

Everything was fine. He was in control. All he had to do was stick with the plan and use Carrie Whelan to get to Travis Whelan, who was his most direct route to Natalie Perez.

And once he got to Natalie...she'd pay. He'd make her pay dearly for what she'd done to him. He'd make them all pay. No one bested Roman Birkenfeld. Not his sanctimonious brother and holier-than-thou sister, not his parents, whom he could never please.

Well, he was pleasing himself now. And he wasn't going to let a woman—one woman, Natalie Perez—bring him down.

Four

Carrie couldn't believe it. Nathan had actually called her again—the very next day—and he'd asked her to go out with him that same night. His aggressiveness was exciting and flattering, and she was going for it.

She picked up the bottle of pricey and very sexy perfume her friend, Stephanie Firth, had given her for Christmas a couple of months ago. With what she felt was an act of daring, she spritzed it across the tops of her breasts. Then she took one final look at herself in the mirror.

The dress was new. It was also black and short and body hugging and cut low enough to show an incredible amount of cleavage.

Resisting the urge to tug the hem down a little

closer to her knees and the square-cut bodice a little closer to her chin—in both cases many, *many,* many inches closer—she slipped into four-inch stiletto heels. The sexy shoes, all slim straps and sleek black Italian leather, were another extravagance. It wasn't often she could even wear heels on a date for fear of towering over the guy.

"Let's face it…it isn't often you get to go on a date, period, thank you very much, Travis," she muttered, then forced herself to steer away from any negative energy—and away from any thoughts of how Ryan might react to the way she looked. He'd probably tell her to put on a sweater.

Well, tonight wasn't about pleasing Ryan. Tonight was her night. Hers and Nathan's. Stephanie was the only one who even knew about their dinner date. Ry showing up at the Royal Diner the other night was just a little too coincidental. She wasn't taking any chance of her brother or Ry sabotaging her evening with some misguided notion that she wasn't capable of making her own choices.

With a sweep of siren-red lipstick that matched her nails and assurances that she was simply being sophisticated, not obvious, she grabbed her coat and headed for the door. She had no intention of keeping Nathan waiting. He'd had a devil of a time carving out a few hours from his schedule at the hospital— that's why they were meeting at Claire's instead of him picking her up. That was fine by her. It would give her a chance to make an entrance.

She wanted to knock the doctor's socks off. If this outfit didn't do it, she didn't know what would. And when the little voice niggling away at the back of her mind tried to tell her she might be making a mistake, that she might be leaping a little too fast, that he might be pushing a little too hard, she made a conscious decision to ignore it.

She was a big girl. She'd always been a good judge of character. Nathan Beldon's character was just fine. So was his smile. He wasn't Ry. But for once and for always, Ry wasn't interested. And Nolan... She stopped herself, horrified, and cursed Ry under her breath. *Nathan* not Nolan. *Nathan* was interested. Very interested. And she and her little black dress were going to make sure he stayed that way.

The wine, Carrie thought, was perfect. The candlelight was romantic and Nelson— She mentally slapped herself over her repeated mental block when it came to Nathan's name and made a promise to slap Ryan, too, the next time she saw him, for planting the seed that refused to die.

Okay. She could do this. *Nathan.* Nathan, Nathan bo-bathen, banana-panna mo-mathan, fe, fi, fo, Nathan. Na-than.

Got it.

Deep breath. Regroup.

She smiled across the table. Reestablished the mood. One more time: the wine was perfect, the candlelight was romantic and *Nathan* was definitely interested.

"Have I told you how incredibly gorgeous you look tonight?" he asked, his gaze flicking from her face to her very-there cleavage then back to her face again.

Assuring herself that his hot looks made her feel desirable, not a little uneasy, she blinked demurely over her wineglass. "Twice. And frankly I can't think of a single reason for you to stop now."

His chuckle was deep and sexy as he lifted his glass toward hers. "To the beginning of a beautiful…friendship," he added after a meaningful pause.

"Yes," she said, ignoring a little flutter of nerves and clinking her glass to his. "To beginnings."

Ry felt like a louse. Hell. He *was* a louse.

"You want to tell me what this is about now?"

He smiled grimly across the front seat of his black Lexus at his friend, Stephanie Firth. The model-slim librarian and high school drama coach was a quietly stunning beauty who had not yet figured out exactly how pretty she was or how to use her shy intellect to intrigue the opposite sex.

He and Steph had been buddies since grade school. These days she wore her light brown hair straight and long. Back then she'd worn it in pigtails and hidden her pretty brown eyes behind owlish glasses. He'd been the class clown, she the class brain who had taken a lot of grief over her intelligence and her tall, gangling frame, which she had since grown into quite nicely.

She used to help him out with geography and he used to knock Josh Bowstead, the class bully, into the scrub brush out back of the middle school playground whenever Josh got a yen to call her egghead or Einsteinette or pencil or bean pole or be a general pain in her easily bruised and very fragile ego.

They'd even tried the dating thing once during their freshman year, then laughed themselves silly over a first kiss that was pretty much all locked braces and sweaty palms. The experience had been enough to satisfy them both that the only chemistry between them involved the notes she'd slipped him so he could study for his chem final. But their bond of friendship had stood up over time and she still turned to him when she was in a pinch...just as he turned to her.

Tonight, however, he was using her. If that didn't make him a louse, his plans to spoil Carrie's date did.

"Why does tonight have to be about something?" he asked evasively as he parked the car. The Lexus wasn't a four-wheel-drive like the trucks and SUVs he favored, but it was one smooth, sleek machine, and he hadn't been able to resist it when he'd seen it on the lot a month ago. You could never have too many horses or too much horsepower, he'd always said. "Can't an old friend take an old friend out to dinner without having to have a reason?"

"Oh, I suppose they could," she said, slicing him a suspicious look as he led her through the front door of Claire's, "but, gee, isn't it coincidental that you had to head straight home after your meeting at the bank, until I told you Carrie had a dinner date with Dr. Beldon, and then suddenly, why, you were just dying for one of Claire's rare filet mignons?"

"Yeah, well—" he cleared his throat of the lump of guilt that had lodged there and forced a smile "—a guy's got to eat."

"Uh-huh," Steph said, telling him with a look that she didn't know what he was up to, but that steak, no matter how well prepared, was not a factor in his motive for bringing her here.

Thankfully, before she could call him on it, the maître d' was escorting them to a table set with sparkling white linen, slim burgundy tapers and fine Austrian crystal.

The moment Ry spotted Carrie and Beldon seated at a secluded table in the corner of the room, the decor and genteel ambiance of Claire's faded to a distant, background buzz.

All he saw was Carrie.

In a killer dress that damn near dropped him to his knees.

The vibrant fire lighting her eyes and brightening her cheeks was rivaled only by the shimmering highlights the candlelight cast in her silky red hair...and by the flames licking through his belly and spreading by slow degrees to his groin.

He'd always thought she was pretty. Had done his damnedest to avoid thinking about the fact that she was also sexy as hell. There was no avoiding it tonight. Not the way she looked.

The creamy swell of her breasts rose and fell provocatively above her almost-there dress as she laughed and, with a flirty tip of her head, showed off the slim, elegant lines of her throat.

My God, she looked incredible. Edible. And Beldon was ogling her as if he wanted to lap her up like ice cream.

No way, Ry decided then and there, was he letting that slug put his clammy hands on her. Not on his woman. Whoa. Strike that. Not on his *watch.*

She was not his woman. Never would be…but she *was* his responsibility. He'd promised Trav.

He'd been a reluctant guardian angel up until this point. Had been telling himself Beldon was harmless. But there was nothing harmless in the man's eyes tonight. He had *predator* written all over him…and Carrie was the most innocent of prey.

Ry might be a louse, but his cause was righteous and had him cutting an arrow-straight path to their table.

"Well, would you look who's here?" he said, faking surprise.

Stephanie shot him a look as he touched a hand to the small of her back and guided her along ahead of him. "What in the devil are you up to, Ryan Evans?" she asked in a hushed whisper.

"Why...just being neighborly, Steph. Just being neighborly."

Carrie wasn't sure what alerted her, but she was aware of Ry's presence before she ever saw or heard him. Each individual hair on the back of her neck had sprung to attention just before his deep baritone voice boomed into the secluded intimacy Nathan had created with his hot looks.

"Aw, look at that, would you, Steph. Don't they look great together?"

No! she thought, refusing to believe Ry had just intruded—again—on her evening with Nathan.

No, no, no! This cannot be happening. Not again.

She closed her eyes, drew a calming breath and assured herself that when she opened them, Ry would be gone, his voice just a figment of her imagination, and all she would see was Nathan's attentive smile.

Only, Nathan wasn't smiling. Instead, his jaw was clenched and that huge vein was bulging out on his forehead again. His face had also turned the color of the wine filling their glasses.

Her heart sank as her temper ratcheted up about a bizillion degrees.

"Can you believe the good luck?" Ry asked in his very best, golly shucks and I'll-be-darned cowboy yokel drawl. "What are the odds of running into y'll two nights in a row?"

"About as good as the odds of you living to see

your next birthday,'' Carrie muttered under her breath before finally shooting a glare up at Ry, who stood by their table sporting a big dumb grin.

Beside him Stephanie looked apologetic and embarrassed and was leaning just a little to the left of mortified.

''Had we known you were coming, we'd have arranged for a larger table,'' Nathan said with a stiff smile. ''What a shame you can't join us.''

As hints went, Nathan's statement was the size of the *U.S.S. Roosevelt.* Carrie silently applauded him for his resourcefulness. Her celebration, however, was short-lived. She should have known it would take the entire U.S. Naval fleet for Ryan to get the message.

''D'you hear that, Steph? The man wants us to join them. Didn't I tell you he was a stand-up guy? Robert,'' Ry said, hailing a passing waiter. ''How about a couple of extra chairs and place settings here? The doc just invited us to dinner. But the tab's on me.

''No, no really,'' he added, deliberately misinterpreting Carrie's glare with a quick, magnanimous grin. ''I insist.''

Carrie sat there and quietly set about plotting murder as Ry made himself comfortable and, with the charm of a snake oil salesman, introduced Stephanie to Nolan.

Nathan.

She rubbed her fingertips to her suddenly throbbing temples. She really was going to have to kill him for this. She just couldn't live with herself if she didn't.

"Third time's the charm," Nathan said later that week as he and Carrie sat huddled on a blanket in the city park. "Evans can't possibly stumble on to us here," he added on a sour note.

They sat in a secluded spot in the park near the lake, and even though the evening was chilly—it was, after all, February—her heart was warmed by both Nathan's thoughtfulness and persistence in the face of Ryan's *coincidental* appearances every time they tried to find some time to spend together.

She wasn't used to the kind of attention Nathan had been giving her. After their disastrous evening at Claire's that had ended early when he'd gotten a beep on his pager requiring that he hurry back to the hospital, he'd continued to call her.

In fact, he'd called her every day, asked her questions about herself, her volunteer work, told her a few things about himself. It was romantic and flattering, and she really wanted to believe he could be the man who represented her future. Maybe he could, if Ry would quit sabotaging all of Nathan's attempts to get intimate.

Not this time, she thought with unwavering determination. No way could he find them here. Tonight, she'd decided, was the night. The champagne was making her bold. She was going to take Nathan home and—gulp—she was going to take him to her bed.

"I really am sorry about Ryan," she said with a shake of her head. "I can't even give you a logical explanation for why he keeps showing up."

Nathan reached for the champagne bottle, refilled her glass. "Obviously, he's jealous of me."

She barely managed to stall an indelicate snort. "Jealous? Ryan? Oh, no. No...I'm thinking it's more like he has this big-brother complex or something going on."

"Big brother?"

She told him then about her parents' death and how Ry's parents had taken her in and how Ryan had stepped into Travis's shoes when Trav had enlisted in the marines.

"How difficult that must have been for you," Nathan said, and draped an arm over her shoulders.

Without warning she felt the sting of tears burn her eyes. Horrified by the unexpected surge of emotions, she blinked them back and let Nathan's kindness warm her.

"This is very nice," she said when his arm tightened slightly.

"And very private," he said with a hint of suggestion in his voice.

Yes. It was private. And romantic. A twilight picnic at Royalty Park was about as romantic as it got, in her book. Despite the cold weather, she loved it. Nathan's romantic Valentine's Day gesture thrilled her.

So did his smile and the goodies—caviar, crackers,

grapes and Brie—that he'd taken the time to pack into the picnic basket.

Everything was perfect. The champagne cut the chill and relaxed her as much as Nathan's compliments.

"Can I kiss you, Carrie?" he asked as a flock of black birds flew gracefully over the lake.

She turned her face up to his, smiled in invitation...and waited for the heart-pounding excitement to fill her breast as he lowered his mouth to hers.

And waited...and waited...and waited as he pressed his lips to hers, groaned deeply and, with an insistent pressure of his tongue, encouraged her to open her mouth for him.

Okay, she thought, trying to get into the kiss with the same enthusiasm he was showing. This was... nice. Sort of. But...where were the fireworks? she wondered as she worked at making herself respond with as much passion as he seemed to be experiencing for her.

You're just out of practice, she assured herself. It had been a long time since someone had kissed her. A very long time. Determined to become fully engaged in the moment, she lifted a hand to touch it to his hair and shifted a little closer as his other arm wrapped around her and drew her flush against him.

She closed her eyes, made herself relax as he laid her back on the blanket and deepened the kiss...that seemed to go on and on and on...and not really in a good way.

Instead, she felt...cheated. Where was the breathless anticipation? The endless longing?

"Let me come home with you, Carrie," he murmured as he dragged his mouth away from hers and pressed kisses along her jaw.

Wet kisses, she thought. Cold kisses that made her shiver...and not from desire. What was wrong with her? She wanted this. She really, really wanted this, and yet, when his hand started an upward glide toward her breast, she clamped her fingers around his wrist and stopped him.

She sat up abruptly, fighting a surge of panic. "Nathan...I...um ..."

She was so embarrassed. Very slowly she lifted her gaze to his...and saw a flash of fury that frightened her.

And then he smiled, and the anger faded so quickly she wondered if she'd just imagined it.

"I'm going too fast, aren't I?" he asked gently.

So gently that she felt like a fool and a loser.

"No," she insisted and moved back into his arms. "I'm...just a little...I'm not very experienced, Nathan," she admitted, and on a flash of insight, told herself that was the reason she was having difficulty responding to him. It was jitters. "I want you to change that," she added with a boldness that shocked her.

His eyes heated again and he leaned forward to kiss her...just as a horse disguised as a dog came bounding out of the woods and with a deep-throated "Woof" launched himself at Nathan's chest.

"What the hell..." Nathan sputtered as the shaggy, smelly furball knocked him to his back and pinned him there, then held him down with his canine teeth hovering dangerously close to his juggler.

Carrie shot to her feet with a scream and bumped the bottle of champagne, which toppled over and spilled down the front of Nathan's trousers.

After one huge lick, the dog lost interest in Nathan's throat. Still straddling him like a WWF wrestler applying a half nelson, the moplike monster alternately slurped at the champagne-soaked blanket and snarfed up the scattered crackers and cheese while his hind feet mutilated the grapes and ground caviar into Nathan's pant legs.

"Oh my God," Carrie wailed...and finally recognized the dog. "Oh. My. God," she repeated, her shock shifting to fury as she whipped her head around to find the Newfoundland's owner, who, she'd known, wouldn't be very far behind.

Sure enough, Ryan Evans burst out of the trees at a slow jog, an appropriately appalled and apologetic look creasing his brow.

"I can't believe this," she ground out as he trotted toward her, a leash in one hand, an empty dog collar in the other.

He stopped short, a little out of breath, as if he'd been giving chase, and gave her a helpless look.

"Man, I can't, either. That sucker threw his collar slicker than an oil spill."

Yeah, right. How neatly coincidental that a dog whose idea of exercise was licking his food bowl, would tug on a leash so hard that he'd break free.

If rage had a tangible form, it would be a cement block and she would be breaking it over Ry's interfering head. "Get Shamu-the-killer-whale dog off him this instant!" she demanded.

Ry was already moving toward the dog, tugging and coaxing—and not very convincingly, she thought—him off Nathan.

Carrie was so mad she couldn't see anything but red. Couldn't hear anything but bits and snippets of Ry's aw-shucks apologies and "Here, let me help you up, Nelson," and "Gee, so sorry about the mess," and "Whoa...that's really gonna stain, huh?" And the ever popular "You're all wet, man. You'd better head home and out of those pants before you catch a chill."

It was all over but for the venomous looks that Nathan threw Ryan as he struggled to his feet. He slanted Carrie a glare, gathered up his blanket and basket and stomped off toward the parking lot and his car.

Several long, humiliating moments passed as she stood there, peripherally aware of Shamu snuffling around for the last of the cracker crumbs and tidbits of cheese while Ry tried to wrestle him into his collar.

"You, uh, okay?" Ry finally asked.

She followed Nathan's car with her gaze until it disappeared from sight, then slowly turned her attention to the one-man romance wrecker and his four-legged accomplice. "Do I *look* like I'm okay?"

Five

What she looked like, Ry thought, was a woman on the verge. Possibly of murder.

He wasn't scared.

Much.

But he *was* pretty pleased with himself. His timing could have been a little better, though. That creep had had his hands all over her, his tongue jammed down her throat by the time Ry had found them, skirted around to the edge of the woods and let Shamu loose with a heartfelt command to "Kill."

Of course Shamu wouldn't kill a toad, so Beldon had never been in any real danger, but the big hairy lummox dearly loved a picnic so Ry had figured it was a pretty good plan. All in all it was—if you didn't count the look on Carrie's face right now.

He could take her anger. He couldn't take her misery. And she was a riled-up mixture of both.

Guilt gradually took the satisfaction out of his victory. Uneasy, he scratched his jaw and tried to figure out where to go from here.

Here was the dilemma. If he offered her a ride home, she'd tell him to go to hell and walk the twenty blocks back to her house. If he said a quick goodbye, he'd up her anger to the boiling point, but she'd probably demand he give her a ride home.

He opted for effect.

"Well...see ya," he said, and with a firm grip on Shamu, who was now panting in doggie adoration at Carrie, turned to go.

He got all of five steps before her clipped, incensed question stopped him.

"That's it? You ruin my Valentine's Day and all you've got to say is 'See ya?'"

He stopped, turned and pretended to consider. "Let me think. Panic. Disorder. Chaos. Yep. I'd say my work here is pretty much done."

His admission of sabotage threw her for all of about two seconds. It threw him, too. He hadn't meant to own up to it...but she looked so miserable standing there, and while he didn't feel any guilt where Beldon was concerned, he hated to see his little Carrie-bear unhappy.

"*Why* are you doing this to me?" she wailed, her fists clenched against her long coltish legs that were covered in snug, faded denim. And she literally shook with outrage; her cheeks had turned pink from the cold and embarrassment. Her hazel eyes were as big as dinner plates and misty with unshed tears.

Oh, damn. Please, don't let her cry. He couldn't stand it if she cried.

He compressed his lips, looked from her to his feet and shook his head. He couldn't do this anymore. He had to explain. Maybe if he were able to convince her that Beldon was bad news—even though he didn't know it for a fact—she'd come around.

"Come on, bear," he said softly. "I'll take you home. We'll talk."

She shot him a fierce glower, heaved a defeated breath then stomped past him toward his SUV. Without a word she jerked open the passenger door and climbed in.

She was sitting there, her arms crossed tightly over her breasts, glaring out the window when he let Shamu into the back then climbed behind the wheel.

He sat there for a moment, trying to figure out how to breach the tense silence when she very quietly said, "Save it, cowboy. Just drive."

The threat was implicit. If he opened his mouth, the only thing that was probably going to come out of it was a couple of teeth when she busted his chops. He'd seen her in action. For a girl she had a helluva right hook—in her teens, she'd used it on Trav once or twice when his teasing had stirred her into a stew pot full of temper.

She was beyond riled at the moment and working

her way toward a full-blown snit. He'd drawn a few broncs in his rodeo days sporting the same kind of attitude she was nursing right now. They'd slam-dunked him into the dirt like he'd been a wet noodle. He'd lived to ride again...but just barely.

He cleared his throat, turned the ignition and, opting for wisdom over valor, he did exactly what the lady had said. He kept his mouth shut and he drove.

"Inside. Now," Carrie ordered when Ry pulled up in front of her house fifteen minutes later after a very silent ride.

"Yes, ma'am," he said obediently, told Shamu to "Chill for a few minutes" and quietly followed her to her front door.

She could feel his eyes on her as she led the way up her front walk. She hoped he enjoyed the view because he wasn't going to be seeing it again anytime soon.

After unlocking the front door, she swung it open and, with a lift of her hand, indicated he should precede her inside. Compliant to a fault, he eased past her...then stood in the middle of her living room, hands on his hips, Resistol tugged low over his brow and waited...looking for all the world like an ad for pro rodeo or Wrangler jeans or Texas tourism, she thought in disgust as she tossed her house keys on the foyer table.

Damn him for being so gorgeous and so clever and so successful in his mission...whatever it was.

Well, she was about to find out and then she was
going to put the skids to it. On the ride across town,
she'd made herself hold her tongue, tried to settle
herself down so when the words came out, they
would be forceful, rational and decisive.

"I have had it," she said slowly, distinctively and
with enough force that he actually looked a little un-
settled. "I've had it with your meddling. With your
play-acting. With the humiliation."

When he opened his mouth, she held up a hand.
"I don't want to hear it."

Wisely, he held his silence.

"I don't want to hear anything you have to say
because there is no explanation in Texas big enough,
good enough or convincing enough to excuse your
actions.

"Now, I want you to listen to me, Ryan Evans,"
she said, marching up and getting right in his face.

"No more good-ol'-boy grins, no more misguided
protector mentality. No more showing up and sabotaging my dates with Nathan Beldon. I'm a big girl
and I can handle myself.

"Now, I've got a pretty good idea that Trav put
you up to this and I know you feel loyalty to him,
but so help me, if you don't butt out of my life and
my business, I will never speak to you again as long
as I live. And Trav's on the short list of dispensable
people, too, so make sure he knows it."

"Carrie—"

"I didn't say you could talk yet. *I'm* talking.

You're still listening. I want to know if you understand what I'm saying to you. A simple nod will do.''

He tugged on his hat brim, set his mouth in a hard line and settled himself with a deep breath.

"Do. You. Un. Der. Stand?" she demanded.

"Oh, yes, ma'am," he said, and she wasn't at all surprised to hear an edge of anger creep into his voice.

Good, she thought. He'd brought this on. Let him have a taste of it, too. It made it that much easier to stay mad at him.

"Make that 'Yes, ma'am, I understand that I am not to interfere with your life because it's none of my business who you see and what you do.'"

He glared at her. "I've said it before. Nothing's changed. You will always be my business."

She ignored the dark insistence in his voice, drew on her anger to stay the course. "Say it, Ry. Promise me you will not so much as draw a breath within thirty feet of me when I'm with Nathan Beldon again.

"*If* I'm ever with him again," she added with a little sinking sensation in her chest. A man could only take so much interference from testosterone-fueled protectors before he packed up his marbles for good and went home. Nathan had probably reached his limit.

"He's not for you, Carrie."

Her mouth dropped open at his outrageous assumption that he knew what was good for her. "That is not for you to decide!'' she countered, frustration fueling the conviction in her words.

She closed her eyes and covered her face with her closed fists on a growl. ''Why can't you just leave me alone?''

There were tears in her eyes when she dropped her hands. ''You don't want me...so why can't you just leave me alone?''

Oh, God.

Oh, God, oh, God. She couldn't believe she'd said that. *You don't want me.* Mortified, she turned her back to him.

Oh, man, Ry thought, his heart breaking at the defeated set of her slim shoulders.

Didn't want her? He suppressed a groan. If only.

Look at her. She was beautiful, intelligent, caring and compassionate...and passionate as all get-out. And right now she was trembling with such an enticing mix of anger and vulnerability he ached with wanting her.

He gently cupped her shoulders and turned her back around to face him. And felt a current of longing and lust shoot through his blood like a freight train.

What sane man wouldn't want her? What flesh-and-blood man couldn't help but want to take her in his arms and kiss away the tear that escaped and tracked down her cheek? What man with an ounce of testosterone in his DNA wouldn't kill to feel the fire of her passion?

He was all of those men…and out of control to boot. Suddenly he couldn't stop himself. With his hands wrapped around her upper arms, he drew her slowly toward him, watching the emotions shift across her face as his left leg wedged between hers, and her full breasts pressed against his chest.

Her eyes shimmered with a mist of unshed tears…and a stunned and needy anticipation. And just that fast he was a goner.

There wasn't a force in the world at that moment strong enough to keep him from lowering his head, touching his lips to hers and losing himself in her giving heat and surrendering sigh.

Wrong, wrong, wrong. The words hammered out from the part of his brain that was still functioning. But function gave way to feeling as he sank into the kiss, opening his mouth over hers, coaxing her lips apart, slipping his tongue inside and diving headlong into heaven.

Sweet.

Lord above, she was so sweet. And sassy and sexy as she rose up on tiptoe, wrapped her arms around his neck and plastered her long, lush body against him like she was a blanket and he was an unmade bed and, heaven help him…he had to stop this now.

But he couldn't. He just couldn't.

It was too good. She was too…everything. Sensual, shy, wanton, wanting. And it made him want, too—like he'd never wanted in his life.

Against everything that was right, he took. He

filled his hands with her tight, tidy behind, lifted and pressed her up and against his erection with a groan that left no question what he wanted and needed for both of them.

He didn't know how it happened, but the next thing he knew he had her backed up against a wall. Her hands had tangled in his hair, knocking his hat to the floor, and their kiss just kept uncovering deeper levels of sensation while his hands tunneled up under her sweater and found bare skin. Silky. Hot. And not nearly enough.

He wanted her naked. He wanted inside of her. He wanted his mouth on her breast, his tongue between her legs. In zero-point-five seconds, she'd taken him from protector to plunderer and there wasn't a single message his rational brain was sending to his libido that was powerful enough to break through the fog of arousal.

So this was spontaneous combustion.

So this was chemistry squared.

So this was...*not* going to happen.

The blood flow finally rerouted back to his brain and cognizant thought made a comeback. With a growl of frustration he lifted his head, sucked in air.

And looked at the face he'd just ravaged.

Her lips were wet and swollen and so pretty and pink; her eyes were glazed, her lush lashes fluttering slowly as if she, too, was trying to get her bearings and figure out what had just happened.

Insanity. That's what had happened. Some cosmic

blip had flashed across his radar screen and short-circuited his brain, hot-wiring him straight into sensual overload.

He wanted nothing more than to dive back in and kiss her again, strip off her clothes, lay her down on the closest horizontal surface and take this to the next level.

And when her soft sigh and desperately whispered ''Ry, please...make love to me,'' drifted through his mind like a drug, he almost...almost...did it.

But this was Carrie.

Little Carrie-bear.

Trav's kid sister.

Trav's *virgin* kid sister.

The truth hit him like a bucket of ice water. *This couldn't happen.* And damn if it hadn't just almost happened in the worst—and best—possible way.

Very carefully, very deliberately, he forced himself to pull away from her, drop his hands and take a step backward.

Damning himself for his lack of control, he stared into her glazed eyes and struggled with the words to set this right.

Only, there were no words to make it right. What he'd done was inexcusable. What he'd wanted—what he still wanted—was not what she needed.

Angry with himself, even a little angry with her for not having the instincts to protect herself from the likes of him or a predator like Beldon, he made an instant decision on how this had to be handled.

It wasn't going to be pretty. It wasn't going to be nice. But it would be effective. And it was necessary.

Carrie swayed on her feet and might have toppled like a tower of children's blocks if the wall at her back hadn't steadied her.

Oh, my.

Oh my, oh my, oh my.

So *that's* what all the fuss was about. That feeling of…of being lost, of being found, of discovering for the first time a yearning so strong it made her knees weak. A desire so intense it made every muscle in her body clench and melt like butter, simultaneously. Helpless longing, endless need…everything she'd been hoping to experience with Nathan.

Everything she'd always known she'd find with Ry.

Make love to me.

She'd barely thought the words and then she'd heard herself saying them out loud.

And then she'd felt him pull away.

And now…now he was glaring at her…like some brooding grizzly. Like someone who didn't even like her, let alone want her.

The passion she'd felt in his kiss had shifted to anger. And she didn't understand.

"Ry?"

"So…do you understand now what happens when you don't behave yourself?"

She blinked, chilled to the bone suddenly, where

only moments ago she'd felt nothing but heat. She clutched her arms around herself, his anger slicing through the last of her longing and heightening her feeling of vulnerability. "*Behave* myself?"

He gave her a stern stare and bent to snag his hat from the floor. "You just got a lesson, little girl...I hope you learned it well."

"A lesson?" She didn't understand. She didn't understand any of this. "What...what are you talking about?"

"I'm talking about what happens when a woman teases a man beyond reason."

He brushed some imaginary dust from the brim of his hat, then settled it jerkily on his head. "I saw the way you let Beldon kiss you in the park. I saw the way you let him put his hands all over you."

For what felt like an eternity, all she could do was stare. She opened her mouth. Closed it. Then finally found her voice. "What does Nathan have to do with what just happened between us?"

He shook his head, then smiled...the picture of tolerant benevolence. "Sweetie...that's what I'm trying to tell you. Nothing happened between us but a little adult-education class."

She felt as if she'd just walked into a theater in the middle of a movie—a horror movie or a foreign movie—French with German subtitles. "Adult education?"

"Exactly. Honey, I just taught you that if that had been Beldon instead of me—someone who cares about you—you'd be flat on your back and compromised by now.''

Time stopped while her mind wrestled with his reaction and his words until finally she pulled it all together.

He hadn't kissed her because he *wanted* her. He'd kissed her because he thought she needed protection from herself when it came to the opposite sex and he needed to show her the error of her ways. He'd kissed her because he thought she hadn't behaved appropriately with Nathan and if he hadn't intervened, she might have ended up, God forbid, *compromised.*

An incredulous laugh pushed out from somewhere in the vicinity of her horribly bruised pride. ''*Compromised? Was that really the word you used?*''

She laughed again, covered her face with her hands, then on a deep breath let them drop. She glared at him. ''What Victorian tome did you pull that out of?''

He actually flinched and turned a shade of red she'd never seen on him before. To cover his discomfort, he shook his finger at her. ''Beldon wouldn't have stopped like I did.''

''So...let me get this in perspective. You kissed me and backed me up against the wall to scare me straight, is that it?''

''Damn right I did. And I hope it worked. If you have an ounce of sense in you, you'll think twice before you—''

"Before I what?" She cut him off, her anger firing with a vengeance. "Before I go out and throw myself at another man's feet and beg him to *deflower* me? Now, there's a word for you. You can probably find it right next to *compromise*."

She sucked in a ragged breath. Dragged her hands through her hair. How pathetic was she? How pathetic was she to actually have thought he had kissed her because he'd wanted her? Because he'd been as excited and aroused and as in love with her as she was with him?

Well. He was right about one thing. She'd definitely learned a lesson: Trust her intellect not her heart. Her head had known weeks ago that she had to give up on him. It was her heart that hadn't been on board with the plan.

Well, it was on board now…bruised and bleeding, but on board. And one shot at this kind of humiliation was all he was going to get at her.

"Get. Out," she ordered, walked to the door on shaky legs and opened it wide.

"Oh, now, bear," he began in that condescending, cajoling voice that made her want to grind her teeth…preferably into some very tender part of his body that created immeasurable pain. "Don't get all huffy. You know this was for your own good."

"I do know," she said with all the sweetness of vinegar and the sincerity of Jerry Springer, as he stepped out the doorway and onto her front stoop, "and I thank you so *very* much for presuming to know what's best for me."

She watched his face as tolerance transitioned to suspicion. "That was um…sarcasm, right?"

"So you *do* have some functioning brain cells," she ground out through a nasty smile, then whipped the door shut in his face.

Ry heard her throw the dead bolt. Heard her snarl of rage. Heard her give in to the tears.

He hung his head, closed his eyes, laid his closed fist against the door…and almost begged her to let him back in.

He wanted to hold her…to tell her the truth. That he was stupid crazy about her. That he hadn't meant to hurt her…that he actually had damn few functioning brain cells left when it came to her or he never would have kissed her in the first place then bumbled out that lamebrain, dull-witted excuse to cover up his mistake.

"Hell, Shamu could have come up with a better story to make sure she didn't read the truth in that kiss. No offense, buddy," he told the dog, who gave him a soulful look when he climbed behind the wheel.

And what *was* the truth in that kiss? The *honest* truth, he asked himself grimly.

He slumped back in the driver's seat. The truth was that the moment he'd touched his lips to hers he'd stopped thinking of her as little Carrie-bear.

She'd become a woman in his arms. A woman whose response had sizzled with instant arousal…and fueled his libido to flash point.

Hell. He was still aroused…his damn hands were shaking.

He wrapped his fingers around the steering wheel to steady them, then stared through the windshield at…nothing.

And came up with nothing.

There was no good answer to the what-ifs that, despite the futility of the situation, had been rattling around in his head since he'd kissed her. Yet they were still forming. What if he *had* made love to her? What if she wasn't Trav's sister? What if she wasn't off-limits because of it…because of a hundred other reasons that didn't add up to what she needed him to be?

He felt as low as the cracked asphalt beneath the wheels of his four-by-four as he turned the key, shifted into Drive and pulled slowly away from her house. Damn Trav for putting him in this position. Damn Beldon for putting the moves on her. And damn the sleepless nights he'd spent agonizing about the possibility of another man making love to her for the first time. And all the times after that.

A fist curled in his gut at the thought. He knew he couldn't be that man. He'd known it for years. Carrie had always had a crush on him. For her sake he'd always done his darnedest to discourage it. Truth-

fully, he'd figured she would grow out of it...
eventually. Her response just now said she hadn't.

He drummed his thumbs on the steering wheel as
he headed across town for the Cattleman's Club and
the bar, where a tall cold one wouldn't substitute for
what he wanted but would give him something to do
with his hands—and his mouth—other than kiss the
one woman he had no business kissing.

He'd never quite understood why she was attracted
to him anyway...had always assumed it might have
had something to do with his rodeo background.
Women seemed to go for rodeo riders, and Lord
knew he'd had his share of fun with the ladies over
the years. But he didn't see himself as any prime
catch—certainly, he wasn't good enough for Carrie.

Yeah, he could take care of her financially. He was
loaded, but that was an accident of heritage, not any
great doing on his part. His granddaddy had struck
it rich in oil and his daddy had kept up the tradition
in real estate. But she didn't need his money, anyway. Trav had seen to it that she'd never want for
anything.

Besides, he'd learned a long time ago that money
didn't make a man...not the kind of man Carrie
needed to make her happy. She needed someone who
wanted to settle down. And that just wasn't him. He
wasn't cut out for home and hearth and sharing at
the end of the day.

At least he didn't think he was, but he figured it
was telling that he'd never held on to a relationship

with a woman long enough to find out. And that was telling in itself. If he was into commitment, it seemed he'd have tried it on for size by now. He wasn't sure he'd be any good at it...or answering to anyone but himself.

He was content alone, if not darn right hunkered in on the Dusty E since his folks had retired from ranching and resettled in Palm Beach. He was happy raising cattle and riding the range with Shamu and setting off on sporadic TCC missions. He liked the solitude—along with the occasional night with a pretty, attentive woman. Although, lately the only pretty woman who came to mind was the woman he'd just left crying.

He'd probably make her cry a lot if he gave in and made love to her. And that was something he just didn't want to do. Carrie deserved an anchor she could stake a future on...and he was still floating with the currents.

Bottom line, she needed someone better than a busted-up former rodeo star who had tried to get into the marines when Travis had but couldn't pass the physical because of all the injuries he'd gotten riding broncs on the high school rodeo circuit.

She needed a guy who would take care of her and protect her from the trouble she was bound to get into if left to her own devices. Beldon being a case in point.

And then there was Trav. Trav was Ry's best friend. If he started something with Carrie, he'd end up losing Trav's friendship—not to mention there was the possibility of getting his block knocked off, and he liked it fine where it was, thank you very much.

He pulled into the TCC parking lot, resolved, if not enthusiastic, about why their first kiss had to be their last.

But damn, did he hate hurting her.

And damn, did he still want that woman.

Six

Carrie stared at her tear-swollen face in her bathroom mirror. Considered writing a big red *L* for loser in the middle of her forehead in lipstick.

But then she got mad.

She did *not* cry. She was not a weeping Wilda, and hated that she'd been reduced to tears by Ryan Evans.

Well, she'd shed her last tear over him.

And she was finished letting him interfere with her life and her plans...on any level.

So what if his kiss had melted her bones.

And, oh, Lord above, had it melted them.

Her knees got weak and she got a muzzy feeling in her tummy all over again just thinking about it.

And then she got mad all over again.

For a moment—one long, blissful, hot, mindless moment—she'd thought Ry was kissing her because he wanted her. His kiss had been a lie. All he was doing was teaching her a lesson, doing his duty—his cursed *brotherly* duty—and warning her away from Nathan Beldon. She was furious that he'd had the gall to accuse her of being a tease. Hurt that he would think of her that way.

So what if his kiss had made her blood boil. He wasn't offering her a darn thing but grief. Nathan...Nathan had been sending all kinds of signals that he was offering more. And Ry Evans or no Ry Evans, she owed it to herself to find out exactly how much more.

She pressed ice-cold water to her eyes, repaired her makeup, then ran a brush through her hair. Quickly exchanging her dark blue sweater for a Valentine-red silk blouse, she grabbed her car keys, and headed for Nathan's apartment across town. It was still early evening. It was still Valentine's Day. And she was not going to spend the rest of the night alone. She was going to go to Nathan, apologize again and make it impossible for him not to take her to bed.

Roman Birkenfeld stood, reached for his trousers and tugged them on. Behind him Marci lay sprawled and spent in the middle of his rumpled bed. There was a bruise on her left cheek he couldn't muster enough conscience to be sorry about. He hadn't

asked her to come over here. It wasn't his fault she'd
been a handy outlet for his fury when he'd returned
from the park, his pants soaked with champagne and
smeared with caviar.

It was Evans's fault. The interfering, clod-kicking
yokel had crossed a line tonight. No one humiliated
Roman Birkenfeld. He felt the rage boil up in his
blood all over again, just thinking about how the
slow-talking and slow-witted Texan had managed to
thwart yet another attempt to get to Natalie Perez
through Carrie Whelan.

He'd almost had her. Almost gotten her to take
him home, when Evan's filthy mutt had attacked him.

Seething with building fury, he stalked into the
living room, snagged his cell phone and dialed.

"Give me a report," he ordered when Jason Carter
answered the phone. "And you'd better have something good to tell me about my money."

He waited with growing impatience as Carter, one
of the muscle men he'd hired to help him track down
the money, handed the phone to Tommy Stokes.

"Nothing new, boss," Stokes said stoically when
he came on the line. "We know one of those Cattleman's Club guys who's been protecting Perez took
the money to their prissy rich man's club, but we
haven't figured out a way to get to it."

"You break into the damn place, is how you do
it," he barked back, at the end of his tolerance with
the entire situation. "How hard can it be to get past
a few *prissy*—wasn't that your word—cowboys?"

"You said you wanted to keep it low-key," Stokes said defensively.

"We're past low-key, you moron. I need that money. And I need it yesterday. Now, find it and bring it to me or your miserable lives aren't going to be worth living."

He punched the end key before Stokes could utter a response, then tossed the phone angrily against the wall. Damn Natalie Perez. Everything had started unraveling when she'd gotten wise to his black-market baby ring.

He raked his hands roughly through his hair, forced a calming breath. And told himself he wasn't coming unglued. He was still in control. It hadn't been his fault that he'd fallen so far behind in his payments to the Atlantic City boys. He'd just had a streak of bad luck at the casinos. That's why he'd started the baby theft in the first place, to pay off his gambling debts.

"Okay. Don't think about that now," he told himself aloud. "Think positive. Stokes and Carter will get the money." The half million in the diaper bag represented all of his hard work—the cumulative amount from the sale of several babies over several months. Once he recovered it, he'd get the heat off his back...and then he'd make a few people pay. Natalie Perez would be first; Ryan Evans, however, was rising to the top of his short list like a bullet.

He was pacing the room, thinking of ways to deal with him when his doorbell rang. He was so

PLAY THE
Lucky Key Game
and you can get

Do You Have the LUCKY KEY?

FREE BOOKS
and a FREE GIFT!

Scratch the gold areas with a coin. Then check below to see the books and gift you can get!

YES! I have scratched off the gold areas. Please send me the 2 FREE BOOKS and GIFT for which I qualify. I understand I am under no obligation to purchase any books, as explained on the back of this card.

326 SDL DVF2   225 SDL DVGH

FIRST NAME

LAST NAME

ADDRESS

APT.#

CITY

STATE/PROV.

ZIP/POSTAL CODE

2 free books plus a free gift

1 free book

2 free books

Try Again!

Visit us online at
www.eHarlequin.com

DETACH AND MAIL CARD TODAY!

(S-D-02/04)

If offer card is missing write to: Silhouette Reader Service, 3010 Walden Ave., P.O. Box 1867, Buffalo NY 14240-1867

BUSINESS REPLY MAIL
FIRST-CLASS MAIL   PERMIT NO. 717-003   BUFFALO, NY

POSTAGE WILL BE PAID BY ADDRESSEE

SILHOUETTE READER SERVICE
3010 WALDEN AVE
PO BOX 1867
BUFFALO NY 14240-9952

NO POSTAGE
NECESSARY
IF MAILED
IN THE
UNITED STATES

lost in thought he didn't even think. He just opened the door.

And stared straight into Carrie Whelan's anxious face.

"Nathan," she said hesitantly. "Can…can I come in?"

Before he could stop her, she shouldered around him and into the apartment.

"I'm so sorry," she said, her hands clenched together in front of her. "It was horrible…what Ryan did. I came to…well…to tell you that if you still want to spend the night with me—"

Her voice trailed off as her eyes strayed, then opened wide and held on a spot just beyond his shoulder.

He knew without turning around what—or who— she saw. He turned, looked over his shoulder and saw Marci standing in the doorway, wearing only his shirt and a catlike smile of triumph.

"Whoops," Marci said with a laugh and disappeared back into the bedroom.

He drew a deep breath and turned back to Carrie who looked as if someone had just gut punched her.

"Carrie…I can explain," he said quickly, confident he could put a spin on this that the gullible little ingenue would buy.

"Not necessary," she said stiffly, and turned for the door.

He snagged her arm, angry all over again, at Marci, at this stupid little doe-eyed girl and the time

and effort he'd had to put into winning her over.
"Please," he said, sounding appropriately desperate.
"Let me explain. It's not what you think."

"Nothing," she said with a pathetic lift of her
chin, "ever is." Then she practically ran out the
door.

Seething, he damned her rotten timing and his bad
luck for getting caught in a little recreational sex.
And then he turned back to the bedroom...blood in
his eyes.

Carrie's hands trembled as she raced across the
parking lot and punched her keyless remote to unlock
her car.

Eyes wide, blinking back tears of humiliation, she
peeled out of the lot and onto Hanover Street.

And then she just drove.

Wanting to deny what she'd just seen...even considering turning around and letting Nathan make his
explanation.

And then she got a clue.

There was no explaining...no matter that Nathan
had snagged her arm and begged her to let him.

What was there to explain? He'd just gotten out
of bed. With his nurse...Mary somebody. Maid...
Mary. Made...Mary. A hysterical laugh burst out.
Mary made quite a statement standing there in nothing but her bed-mussed hair and Nathan's rumpled
shirt.

"What, do I have a sign on my back, or something?'' she asked skyward. ''Humiliate me. Lie to me. Fool me. I love the abuse. Pile it on. I can take it.''

And then she wasn't laughing anymore. She was crying. Damn it, she was crying again! Like she never cried. Like she hadn't cried since that awful time when her parents had died. Huge, racking sobs flooded her vision and made her throat ache and made her feel spineless and pathetic. Because she *couldn't* take it. Didn't understand why she had to.

He'd been right. Ry had been right. Nathan was a loser. He'd just been...what? Using her?

She wiped the back of her wrist over her cheek and under her nose. ''But why? To what purpose?

''And why me,'' she demanded bitterly. Or maybe the questions was, Why not me? Why, just once, couldn't something work out for her in the love department?

All she wanted was someone special. All she wanted was someone to love. To make a life with. To make babies with. To replace the family she'd lost when she'd been little more than a baby herself.

And all she'd ever gotten was interference from her brother and now Ry...and from fools who either ran or didn't care enough to make a difference in her life.

Hours later she'd left the city lights behind and was cruising down miles of empty highway. She wasn't even aware when she'd crossed the Royal city limits. Wasn't conscious of the fact that she'd taken the old Cattle Trail Road. She'd just driven. Mile after mile after mile.

It was after midnight when she pulled into the main drive of the Dusty E. And it wasn't really a surprise, when five minutes later, she cruised to a stop in front of the Evans's ranch house.

She might not have deliberately set out for the Dusty E, but her subconscious had led her to the one place she'd always felt safe. Home.

Yeah. She'd come home, she realized as she cut the motor and killed the lights. Then she just sat there and let the darkness and the sense of open arms settle around her like a warm, cuddly blanket. She'd been an orphan when Ry's mom had welcomed her into the rambling tan stucco house with its graceful, open veranda and endless banks of arched windows. She'd been brokenhearted then. She was brokenhearted now.

And this place—filled with fond memories that had become her safe haven all those years ago—had drawn her like a combat-weary soldier was drawn to home.

She let out an exhausted breath and, leaning forward, pressed her forehead against the back of her hands, which were gripped around the top of the steering wheel.

And felt another overwhelming wave of grief wash over her.

She'd come home to lick her wounds...and yet the

man who had caused the deepest cut to her pride was even now, sleeping in the bedroom behind the fourth window to the right of the entryway.

Tired to the bone, she sat there for several moments…then lifted her head and squinted toward the house when the porch light flicked on.

The front door eased opened and Shamu tiptoed out. The big coward, she thought, finally managing a watery grin. This was no watchdog, cautiously sniffing the air. Clearly, he was hoping his master was going to handle whatever critter had decided to risk life and limb to trespass on hallowed Evans ground.

And then Ry stepped outside. She wasn't grinning anymore.

He was shirtless, barefoot and barely tucked into a pair of work- and wash-faded jeans that hung precariously low on his lean hips.

Without her sanction, her heart skipped several beats, and she accepted that it wasn't only home, but Ry who had drawn her here.

He was, she told herself bleakly, the most beautiful man in Texas, with his dark hair mussed and falling over his brow, his brown eyes piercing hers with concern and questions as he walked slowly toward her car.

''Bear? What's up, sweetie?''

She just couldn't help it. When he leaned down, a concerned and sober scowl on his face, she started crying again. Hot, silent tears that trailed down her face and tracked under her chin, and ran, like a salty river, over the convulsing cords at her throat to wet her blouse.

She cried for all the things she'd lost when her parents died. She cried for all she'd lost when she'd finally accepted Ry didn't love her. She cried for her lost pride and Nathan Beldon's betrayal.

When Ry opened the driver's-side door and, without a word, lifted her out of her car, she wrapped her arms around his warm, strong neck and took solace in his softly murmured, ''Shh. Shush now. Don't cry, bear. Don't cry, baby. I've got you.''

And she kept right on crying.

It was killing him.

Ry couldn't stand it. He couldn't stand to see her in this much pain and know he was probably the cause of it. The Carrie he knew was strong. The little girl who had mourned for her parents had grown into a self-contained woman who would feel diminished and embarrassed by giving in to tears. She'd consider it a weakness. Unlike some women he knew, she would never resort to weeping to manipulate a man or get her way. If she cried, then she was hurting. Hurting bad. It took him back to that horrible time when the only thing he could do to help her was be someone for her to hold on to in return.

Wincing as a bare foot met with a piece of gravel, he carried her into the house, kicked the front door closed behind him and headed for the living room.

Still holding her in his arms, he sat down on the

sofa, then settled her onto his lap as her long, sleek body curled into his and clung.

And felt his guilt over the scene at her apartment settle like a festering thorn.

Only the full moon peaking through the huge picture window to the west illuminated the room, casting them in soft shadows and cocooning them in the intimacy of the night. Despite feeling like the horse's ass he was, he was very aware of her slim hip nestled into his lap, far too aware of her warm breast pressing against his chest through the thin red silk of her blouse. But most of all, he was conscious of how badly she needed the very person who had driven her to this state to be her friend right now. A friend...not a man whose first and basic instinct was to comfort her in the most elemental and pleasurable of ways.

It broke his heart to feel her slim shoulders tremble, to feel the warmth of her silent tears on his skin. So he just hung on tighter. Pressing his lips to the top of her head, he combed his fingers through her silky hair and made soothing sounds to settle her.

Her eyes were red and swollen when she finally lifted her head and pressed the heels of her hands to her eye sockets. He watched in silence as her throat convulsed and she made a concentrated effort to pull out of her funk.

"Hold on a sec," he said and, easing her off his lap, walked out of the room. When he returned, she'd done when he'd known she would do, what he'd known she needed a moment alone to do. She'd used the time to compose herself.

He handed her a glass of water and a box of tissue.

"I am too—" a hiccupy shudder broke up her words "—too pathetic to draw breath."

Despite her misery, he smiled. "And you've reached this conclusion all by yourself? Or did someone or something nudge you in that direction?"

She sniffed, then blinked and after a long drink of water, tugged a tissue from the box and blew. "Someone *and* something," she said, mopping up the beautiful mess she'd made of her face and reaching for another tissue.

He didn't even hesitate. He sat back down beside her and drew her onto his lap again. She snuggled into him like a sleepy kitten, looping her arms around his neck and nestling her head under his chin. Her breath was warm against his chest, her fingers cool where they linked together on his bare shoulder.

He circled her hips with his arms and propped his chin on the top of her head. "Want to just hit me and get it over with?"

"Hit you?"

"For being such an ass."

"Well, you can't help what you are."

"Um...ouch." But he was grinning at the return of her spunk as he rubbed a hand up and down her arm. "I'm sorry for making you cry like this."

"Don't flatter yourself. This isn't about you."

He didn't know which emotion was stronger. Relief or bafflement. "So...you wanna tell me about it?"

"What? So you can say I told you so?"

There was more resignation than anger in her words. And suddenly he knew. Beldon.

"What did he do to you?" he asked with barely leashed rage. "If that rat bastard so much as laid a finger on you against your will, I will personally see to it that for the foreseeable future, the good doctor won't be able to manage even simple daily tasks—such as blinking, breathing, or eating—without the aid of a professional health care specialist."

She sniffed out a little laugh. "Relax, Rambo," she said quietly. "He did nothing to me...but by the way his nurse looked when she came slithering out of his bedroom, I'd say he managed to do plenty to her."

He only heard one word. "Bedroom? What were you doing in Beldon's bedroom?"

"That's what I'm trying to tell you. Nothing. I did *nothing* in his bedroom. After you left, I went over to his apartment with every intention of going to bed with him...but there wasn't any room for me there. It seems that 'Nelson' Beldon had a very packed schedule today," she added acidly. "Seduce the town virgin in the afternoon, take his nurse to bed at night."

Ry opened his mouth. Closed it. What would have come out was a short, concise expletive that would have succinctly summed up his opinion of Beldon but would have shocked her virgin ears.

"What's wrong with me?" she began, with such a puzzled, pained look his heart did a little more breaking. "What's wrong with me that I can't attract a man who will stand up to Travis or even have enough strength of character to—"

"Hey," he said, cutting her off. "There is *nothing* wrong with you. Absolutely nothing."

The breath she let out was long and heavy. It nestled her left breast deeper into his ribs, made the fine hair dusting his pecs flutter, made his skin burn.

"Then why can't I find someone to love me?"

Oh, God. He closed his eyes, felt the liquid warmth of a single tear spill onto his chest then trickle down to catch on his nipple. Despite her misery, he flashed on an image of her mouth lapping against his skin, licking that tear away.

He squeezed his eyes shut, tried to force the image from his mind...fought not to think about how lush and soft she was, how the only thing separating her skin from his was a layer of silk and a thin thread of common sense that was unraveling with the same speed as the blood rushing to pool at his lap.

"Is it...is it that I'm not pretty enough—"

"Stop," he interrupted hoarsely. Then dug deep for the right things to say, the right thing to do, when every red blood cell in his body screamed at him to show her right here, right now, just how pretty she was. Just how pretty he could make her feel. And how good he could make both of them feel.

"Beldon's a jerk, all right? Don't let what he did or didn't do diminish the person you are. If a man loves a woman, how she looks is not what's important. It's who she is. It's her mind. Her heart. It's how she lives her life."

She sat up slowly, met his eyes with a slow blink of uncertainty, then smiled sadly. "I get it. What you're saying is that I'm the quintessential blind date. 'I'll set you up with Carrie. She's got a great personality. So, she's a little too tall. A little too thin. Her breasts aren't—'"

"Stop it. You are not too tall or too thin. You are perfect. Your breasts are beyond perfect," he said without thinking...then couldn't help himself and lowered his gaze to the front of her blouse where the plump fullness of the breasts in question pressed against red silk. And then he couldn't stop looking as he gave in to a moment of intense, uncontrollable madness. "Your breasts are...dream worthy. Do you have any idea how many nights I've dreamed about—" He stopped abruptly, a weak wave of sanity returning with the thimbleful of blood that found its way back to his brain.

He closed his eyes. Let his head fall against the back of the sofa. Swallowing convulsively, he mentally kicked himself for his stupidity.

"You...you've dreamed about my...breasts?" she whispered breathlessly.

He made himself open his eyes and look at her. "Lord, yes," he confessed, the line between lucidity and lunacy growing blurry.

Her eyes were alert now...and a little misty. With excitement, with surprise...with a stunned expectancy that suddenly made her bold and her voice as seductive as velvet. "What did you dream, Ry?"

Slowly he shook his head. Tried...really tried...to bring his libido back to heel. "Not a good idea, bear."

"What did you dream?" she insisted in a voice made soft by wonder and by a woman's deadly keen insight that evidently told her he was weakening and fading fast.

Then he was no longer fading. He was gone. Beyond gone...and he didn't even try to resist. Not the hungry look in her eyes, not the element of suspense that with one thought warned him this was wrong, but tempted him beyond reason with another.

In a hushed and raspy voice, he surrendered. "I dreamed about watching you unbutton your blouse for me."

He watched her face, watched the hesitant longing darken her eyes...then held his breath when she lifted her hands and with trembling fingers, started undoing the buttons.

He should stop her. He knew he should stop her. But he was only so strong. And he'd been fighting the good fight where this woman was concerned for what seemed like a millennium.

Her head was down when she reached the last button...so were the last of his defenses. She slowly lifted her gaze to his. ''What else did you dream, Ry?''

Her voice was as hushed as a sigh, but there was a boldness in her eyes that promised him everything...if only he'd ask.

And there was another problem.

Asking was beyond him now, too.

''Take it off,'' he ordered on a harsh whisper.

Seven

She'd been wrong about so many things lately, Carrie thought as she sat on the lap of the man she had loved for so long. She'd been wrong about Nathan Beldon. She'd been wrong about her feelings for him. She'd never come close to loving him. Never come close to this breathless anticipation she felt as Ry's chocolate-brown eyes fired beyond warm to barely banked desire.

And she'd been wrong, she realized with a victorious sense of wonder, about the effect she had on him.

He wanted her.

He was dying to have her.

And she'd never been so glad to be wrong about anything in her life.

Riding on a surge of power the knowledge fostered, her gaze locked on his face as he watched her peel back the sides of her blouse then slowly shrug it off her shoulders.

Beneath the red silk she wore a black satin demi-bra edged in delicate lace. Her breasts spilled over the top of the cups with every deep breath she drew. Just below her left breast, she could feel the elevated beat of her heart. She wondered if he could see it hammering there. Wondered if he knew what his thrilling order had done to her.

His throat worked hard as his gaze shifted from her face then back to her breasts again. ''Now the bra.''

The dark intensity of his command sent a shiver of anticipation eddying through her body, heating her blood, but not once did she consider denying him. She reached behind her back for the clasp, unintentionally arching and thrusting her breasts toward him.

He sucked in a slow breath, and she felt his hands on her hips, felt his fingers digging into her flesh...as if he was fighting to anchor his hands there when he wanted them somewhere else.

She felt shy suddenly as the clasp gave and she slowly lowered the bra away from her body. Shy and brazen and...oh, my...beautiful as she read the heated reaction in his eyes.

It was so much suddenly...so much sensation, so much sensitivity. She couldn't filter it all. Her skin felt flushed and on fire beneath his adoring gaze. Her nipples tightened painfully.

Too fast, she thought as sensations assaulted her with the speed and strength of a lightning strike. And too late to do anything but hang on for the ride, she realized as he stole her ability to breathe, let alone think, when he lifted her until she straddled his lap.

Her hands involuntarily clutched the hot, bare breadth of this shoulders. Her knees dug into the sofa on either side of his hips. The most feminine part of her pressed against the very solid evidence of his desire. Her bare breasts were on a level with his mouth…she could feel the warmth of his breath pulse in an irregular rhythm against her.

And it made her ache.

It made her burn.

Endlessly.

So did his hands, as he slid them up her ribs to cup and adore and stroke her swollen nipples with a caress so tender, yet so needy, a soft plea escaped her parted lips.

"Please," she heard herself whisper just as he bent his head and surrounded her with the hot, wet pleasure that was his mouth.

The first touch of his tongue stole her breath. The gentle suction of his lips made her moan. And the sight of his dark head bent to her breast in the moonlight made every part of her that was woman appreciate the elemental and incredible mystery that was man.

Oh. Oh how she'd wondered. How she'd yearned and ached with the need to know, firsthand, what it felt like to have a man's mouth touch her there...how she'd imagined what it felt like when her nipple changed from velvet soft to diamond hard. And always it had been Ry's mouth she'd fantasized about. Ry's dark hair shifting between her fingers as she held him to her breast, let him suckle and feast and feed on the insatiable hunger he seemed to have for the taste of her.

It was so good. So incredibly good to hear his gruff sounds of pleasure, to watch his mouth open wide and take her in as he went wild for her...so wild his fingers bit into her hips and he pulled her closer, needing more of her.

"You...make...me...crazy." His voice was a low growl against the inside of one breast as he kissed and licked his way to the other. "You...taste... like...heaven," he murmured and bit her lightly before licking away the sting then rimming her areola with his tongue.

It all became a lovely, thrilling, and wondrous blur after that. She was aware only of sensations, was steeped in them, lost in him...in the feel of his mouth touching her everywhere, coasting from breast to breast, racing along the line of her throat, tracking kisses across her jaw, then moving to her mouth to kiss her deeply and sweetly. All the while his big, working man's hands moved gently over her body, unzipping her slacks, sliding them and her panties down her hips.

"Beautiful," he murmured as he laid her back on the sofa and settled his long length beside her. His fingers brushed lightly over her curls, stirring lush longings, awakening carnal cravings she'd never known were a part of her. More than a part of her. They were driving her now. She couldn't help herself...she arched into his touch not knowing what she was asking for...only knowing that she needed.

He knew. He knew exactly what she needed, she realized as he deftly found the center of her, delved deeply with his fingers and made them both moan. She was wet and swollen and the way he touched her...with reverence and desire and such gentle skill...had his name breaking from her lips on a sob.

It was everything she'd ever imagined, things she'd never dreamed, when he finally rose above her, guided himself to her opening and slowly pushed inside her. The pain was sharp, brief, then gone as he filled her where she hadn't before realized she felt so empty.

In that one amazing moment, she knew she was everything to him and that knowledge almost... almost...transcended the exquisite pleasure of his slow and luxurious glide in and out of her body.

Nothing had ever felt so right. Nothing had ever felt so good. With instincts as old as time, as natural as the moonlight spilling through the windows, she wrapped her ankles around his hips and rode with him toward everything wonderful in the night. A building urgency boiled up inside her, then raced on a deliciously sharp edge of heightening sensation.

He'd led her sweetly to this moment, led her expertly and unerringly toward release. Yet when the climax ripped through her, she was unprepared. Like the tributaries of a flood-swollen river that gathered at one predestined point to spill into the sea, a thousand little pleasures peaked and swelled then met with the force of a storm at the spot where their bodies joined.

"R-R-Ryannnn." His name eddied out on a stunned and amazed rush. She clung to him for dear life while her world exploded on a maelstrom of bliss she'd never known, never dreamed existed.

Ry had lost all power of reason the moment she'd brazenly reached behind her back, unclasped her bra and her breasts had spilled from black silk into the shadowy darkness of the moon-drenched night. Had hadn't had a rational thought since. And when she clenched around him, cried his name on a jagged spill of breath, he'd never heard anything so honest or erotic in his life.

With her long legs clasped around his hips and her internal muscles gripping him from within, he drove deep one last time, then rode with her on the most incredible rush he'd ever experienced.

He gritted his teeth, buried himself deeper, utterly spent, completely wasted and inexorably humbled by her unbridled and unrestrained passion. She'd offered him everything. Held back nothing. And given him the world.

He closed his eyes and savored the aftermath. She was so soft. Her hair. Her sighs. Her beautiful breasts. The delicate skin of her belly, where even now she held the weight of his hips without complaint and ran her fingers in a lazy, exhausted caress up and down his spine.

As they lay in the dark, their heartbeats settling, their breaths evening out, he knew there were a lot of things he should be feeling. At the top of the list was guilt. He'd just stolen the innocence of someone he cared about; he'd just betrayed his best friend's trust.

But the damage was already done.

And he hadn't had his fill of her yet.

If the soft, kitten sounds she made when he finally hauled himself off her, then lifted her in his arms and carried her to his bed were any indication, she hadn't had her fill of him, either.

There would be time…lots of time, for guilt in the morning. But there were only so many hours left in this night. He intended to spend every one of them giving her pleasure.

Carrie lay on her back and grinned at the ceiling of Ry's bedroom. She couldn't quit smiling. She'd lost her virginity. Finally.

And it had been—she gave an all-over body stretch—heaven.

It had been…life altering.

It had been…Ry who had made it so wonderful. Twice.

She turned her head on the pillow. Beside her, in the deepest part of a night that the moon had drenched in golden light, he slept. Sprawled spread-eagle on his stomach, the sheet riding low around his hips, he looked the picture of hedonistic indulgence. And, oh…had he indulged. Mostly he'd indulged her.

She clamped her legs together as a now-familiar ache—an ache his passionate loving had created—pulsed there. She supposed she should be exhausted. Instead she felt energized. From everything she'd read, she should be sore. And she was…a little. But not enough to keep her body from quickening with renewed desire and wanting to experience more, needing to learn more…like what pleased him, what excited him. Although, it seemed all she had to do was breathe and maybe stretch her arms over her head and that was enough to make his eyes darken to midnight and his hands grow rough and needy.

Hiking herself up on an elbow, she clutched the sheet to her breast and turned onto her side so she could watch him. Bless you, moon, she thought with a smile as it illuminated the room like a golden twilight, allowing her full visual access to his sleeping form. There was nothing about him that didn't fascinate her. His back was so broad. His skin was so smooth and tanned, and beneath it lay muscles that contracted when she ran her hands over him. Like she wanted to run her hands over him now. All over him.

"Like what you see, do you?"

Her gaze shot upward from his hips to see he'd cracked one eye open and was watching her.

There was mischief and seduction blended with the sleep-gruff huskiness in his tone. Feeling brazen and confident of her new, devirgined status, she made a very un-virginlike move.

Grasping the sheet where it covered his hips, she peeled it slowly away, until his tight, muscled buns and thick strong thighs were completely uncovered.

"Like it even better now," she said, and boldly ran her hand along his leg, from his knee upward around the curve of his buttocks.

He closed his eyes, sank deeper into the bedding. "You're playing with fire, little girl."

"Oh, yeah? Well, I happen to have it on good authority that you've got a hose big enough to put it out."

The minute she'd said it, she clamped a hand over her mouth. Felt her face turn ten shades of red. With very deliberate movements, she eased onto her back and, mortified, pulled the sheet up over her head and held it there.

The bed shook with his chuckle. "Wanna run that by me again?"

"Noooo. Oh, help. I can't believe I said that," she groaned, her words muffled by the sheet.

He laughed again as the mattress shifted and dipped and she felt the warmth of his lean body nestle up beside her.

He tugged on the sheet.

She held it fast. "I'm being embarrassed here. Don't bother me."

His index finger drew coaxing circles around her navel through the sheet. "If you come out...I'll let you play with my hose."

When she shrieked, he burst into laughter. It was contagious. She was laughing, too, when she lowered the sheet and tucked it beneath her breasts. That didn't mean she wasn't still embarrassed.

"Well...*obviously,* I need a little more practice with my pillow talk."

"How about this?" He rose up on his elbow and gave her a slow, deep kiss. "You need a little more practice with this, too?"

She turned toward him, wrapped an arm around his ribs at the same time he threw a muscled thigh across her hips. "I don't think I'll ever have enough practice with that."

His mouth curved into a smile against hers. "Lucky for you, I'm a very patient instructor."

"Lucky for me," she agreed as he opened his mouth wide over hers and delved inside with his tongue.

It was magic, his mouth. The way he could move it over hers with such hunger and skill...it made her heartbeat quicken. Made her blood pulse in places that retained rich memories of the pleasure he'd given her in the night. She couldn't imagine anything better than the way his mouth moved over hers.

But then he started moving his kisses lower. To her breast. To her belly. Her eyes went wide, a little shocky when she realized his intent.

"Let me," he whispered against the silk of her inner thigh when she clamped her legs together in an involuntary reaction to her growing sense of vulnerability.

"Let me," he whispered again, this time a gentle, insistent command.

He kissed her hip point, ran his tongue down the sensitive groove where leg met body and with persuasive pressure and husky assurances, pushed her thighs apart and settled his shoulders between them.

And then he showed her the real magic of his mouth. With skilled fingers, he parted her feminine folds. With murmured praise, his warm breath whispered against her swollen flesh. With a single-minded dedication that sent her heart rate soaring and stalled her breath on a keening sigh, he surrounded her with wet heat and the electric glide of his tongue...and introduced her to the true wonder of being selflessly loved by a man.

West Texas was known for its brilliant sunsets. Sunrise could be a full-blown religious experience, as well. The colors painting the sky this morning rivaled any Ry had ever seen as he stood, fully dressed in jeans, flannel shirt and boots, staring out the kitchen window listening to the coffee perk. But the canvas of brilliant apricots, golds and lavenders splashed along the eastern horizon were lost on him. His mind was full of Carrie.

The red of her hair, the dusky brown of her sensitive nipples, the creamy ivory tone of her skin…especially the skin covering her belly and the inside of her silky thighs. His senses were steeped in the scent of her, in the sounds she'd made when he'd made love to her, the uninhibited joy she'd discovered in her sensuality.

Everything about last night had been incredible. Everything about her had been wonderful.

And everything had been wrong.

Jaw clenched with self-condemnation and guilt, he swore under his breath and called himself ten kinds of fool. He never should have started with her, but once he had, he hadn't been able to stop. *Inexperienced, untutored, virginal*…even one of the three words that had applied to her should have been enough to make him put on the skids. Combined, there was more than enough reason to curb his baser instincts. But with Carrie, what should have been deterrents were unbelievable turn-ons. She'd been so hungry to know…so willing to learn…so incredibly responsive to the slightest touch.

Inexperienced, untutored, virginal. Now she was none of those things. He'd taken them all away from her.

With movements of automation, he reached for a mug, filled it, then resumed his study of the breaking dawn. And tried to figure out where to go from here.

By the time he heard her soft footsteps on the terra-cotta tile of the kitchen floor a few minutes later, the time for figuring was over. He knew what he had to do.

He turned slowly, schooled his face into a blank sheet of paper...and felt his heart hit the floor when he saw her.

He wasn't sure where she'd found that shirt; it was old and blue and soft from many washings. And it had never looked like that on him.

She was all long, golden legs and demure smiles...and when she lifted a hand and shoved her hair from her face, revealing that Whelan cowlick that entranced and fascinated him, it was all he could do to keep from marching her backward toward his bedroom and tumbling her onto the mattress covered in tangled sheets and the scent of her.

He knew what she wanted. A "hello lover" smile. Open arms. Reassurances that last night was as wonderful for him as she obviously felt it was for her.

And she deserved all of that and more. But all he could manage was a grim scowl and what he felt was the right, if not the best, resolution to atone for his mistake. "We need to get married."

Eight

Carrie felt liquid and languid and pretty darn pleased with her new status as an experienced woman when she eased out of Ry's bed that morning. She stretched, and smiling at the memories, ran her hands gingerly over some wonderfully tender spots. It was then she realized all her clothes were in the living room.

It was a long way to walk birthday-suit naked on the morning after the most incredible night of her life. She shouldn't be shy...not after the things they'd shared. The things they'd done. But even as she stood there, knowing Ry could come walking back into the bedroom at any moment, even knowing he knew her body more intimately than she did, she felt a warm flush of color creep through her blood and heat her skin.

His closet seemed like her best option. She snagged the first shirt she found, held it to her face and breathed in the scent of clean and Ry. As she slipped it on, she figured she should probably worry about her hair, but just then the only thing she was worried about was catching Ry before he left the house to start his workday. She needed to see his face. Look into his eyes and find the same love and longing she felt for him.

So when she walked into the kitchen and saw him standing there facing the sunrise—his broad shoulders wrapped in dark flannel, his lean hips tucked into work-worn jeans—her heart did that little stutter step it had been doing for years whenever she saw him. Only, this time she knew why it fluttered so. He was her lover. And he'd made her feel things she'd never dreamed possible.

Something must have alerted him to her presence. His shoulders tensed in the moment before he set his coffee mug on the counter. When he turned, she was smiling…feeling a blood-quickening mix of sweet anticipation and morning-after uncertainty. An uncertainty that grew when his beautiful face remained a mask of unreadable emotions.

She touched a hand to her hair, nervous suddenly and not knowing why.

Until he spoke.

"We need to get married."

She stared at the mouth that had been soft and sensual and needy in the night. This morning it was set in a hard, tense line—yet still, some part of her brain waited for the *Good morning, lover. Last night was fantastic. I can't get enough of you. Let's start all over again.*

But this was no lover's face meeting hers. This was a face set with bleak resolve and there was nothing—nothing in his eyes, nothing in his stance—that said one word about love.

"I'm sorry?" she said, certain she must be seeing this wrong, must have heard him wrong. Certain her ears were still ringing from the incredible rush of her last orgasm and garbling the reception to her brain.

He swallowed thickly, looked beyond her to some spot on the wall that held his rapt attention. "We need to get married," he repeated with grim determination.

Grim. With a capital *G.*

Need to get married.

She shook her head. "What are you talking about?"

And why aren't you saying something like *I love you. I want to marry you. I've been a fool to have denied my feelings for so long.*

But he wasn't saying any of those words. In fact, he wasn't saying anything at all. And the longer he stood there, stone-faced and stoic, the clearer it became that he wasn't thinking those words, either.

Everything that had felt soft inside her hardened.

Everything that felt full to bursting with love deflated like a blown tire. And the optimist in her that had clung to notions of romance and happily ever after finally knuckled under to defeat.

"*Need* to get married? *Need* to?" she repeated, incredulous, suddenly seeing what was happening here.

She'd thought he'd made love to her because he was in love with her. The sad truth was she had practically forced him into it. She'd cried all over him. For Ry, a man who couldn't stand to see anything or anyone in pain, it was like an open invitation to make it all better.

And being a man, he'd done what any man would do when a woman blubbered all over him. He'd given in to his physical urges and his helplessness over her tears and tried to make everything better. With sex.

Now he was sorry.

Now he was playing the martyr.

They *need* to get married. Not because he loved her. Because he'd ruined her.

God. She couldn't believe it.

She couldn't believe she could continue to be so stupid where this man was concerned. And there was no way she was going to humiliate herself again by letting his motives reduce her to tears. She'd done more than enough crying, thank you very much.

"We don't *need* to do anything," she informed him firmly and, turning on her heel, stormed out of the kitchen. She had to get out of here. She had to get out of here now.

She was hunting up her clothes, jerking them on piece by piece when he walked into the living room.

"Carrie, listen."

"Oh, I am so through listening to you." She zipped her slacks, spotted a boot beside the sofa and tugged it on before hobbling across the room to retrieve the other.

"I'm not going to be your ultimate sacrifice, Ry," she announced as she shouldered by him, buttoning her blouse on her way to his front door. "And don't worry. I won't tattle on you to big brother. You're off the hook on that one."

He caught the door before she could slam it behind her. Caught her arm when she would have walked away.

"Carrie—"

"Okay, look," she said, rounding on him. "I put you in a bad position last night. I never should have come out here. But hey...you ended up doing me a big favor, okay? So lose the bad-dog face. You performed like a pro. A girl couldn't ask for more on her first time. Thanks for the great lay, Ry. You were incredible."

She was battling angry tears when he grabbed her other arm and shook her.

"Stop it. Stop it right now. It wasn't that way and you know it."

"Well, what way was it?" she demanded, making

herself look him in the eye. "You want to marry me because you *love* me? Is that what you're trying to tell me?"

Some little part of her—that stupid, childish dreamer—still hoped he'd say yes. Yes, I love you.

But he didn't. Instead he turned pale, wouldn't meet her eyes.

And it hurt. It hurt so bad.

"Well." She squared her shoulders and wrapped what was left of her pride around her. "Guess that look says it all. Goodbye, Ryan. It's been...swell."

His hands tightened on her arms.

She felt very tired suddenly. "For God's sake... would you just let me go with what little dignity I have left?"

He let out a weary breath. "You don't understand. I didn't use any protection. There could be a baby," he said softly.

The words felt like a knife piercing her heart. So that was working on him, too. The old "do the right thing" credo of the incurably macho club. Guilt had prompted his proposal if *We need to get married* could, by any stretch of the imagination, be considered a proposal.

"Yes, there could be a baby," she agreed, lifting her chin, clinging by a fingernail to her self-respect. "I'd love to have a baby. But I won't raise a child with a man who doesn't love me. So either way— you're out of the loop on this one. Now, let me go. Please."

He was quiet for a very long time before finally releasing her.

She didn't wait for him to have another go at her. She got in her car and left.

In her rearview mirror, she saw him standing there, watching her drive away. She didn't see the bleakness in his eyes or hear the soft curse he leveled at himself. She was too steeped in her own misery to recognize his.

Besides being a good friend, Stephanie Firth had a sympathetic ear. Carrie had evidently looked as if she needed both when she'd shown up for her volunteer shift at the library late the next afternoon, just before the library closed at five.

Stephanie had taken one look at her, hustled her into her office, sat her down in the closest chair and shoved a cup of mocha latte into her hands.

"Okay. What's up?" Steph asked gently, perching on the corner of her desk.

With no more prompting than Steph's sympathetic look, Carrie spilled her guts—starting with giving up on her longtime feelings for Ry, to her determination to find a meaningful relationship with Nathan and working right on through everything that had happened since. Including the night she'd spent with Ry. And the disastrous morning after.

"Oh, Lord, he didn't really say that." Stephanie moaned. "Did he?"

Carrie let out a breath that ruffled the hair falling

over her forehead and met Stephanie's frown over her recounting of Ry's *We need to get married* edict.

"Not only did he say it, he meant to follow through on it. The big jerk. As if I'd ever be comfortable playing the part of a ball and chain hanging around his neck."

"Oh, sweetie…he would never think of you like that."

"But I would. *I* would," Carrie repeated.

She shook her head and with a gusty sigh, rested her chin on her palm. "What is it with us, Steph? It's not like we're asking for that much. Why don't we have what it takes to attract a good man who will adore us twenty-four-seven and make us feel like sex goddesses to boot?"

They both grinned, because, really, what else was there to do at this point?

"Hey," Stephanie said, feigning indignation and working to lighten the mood, "there is no *we* anymore. I'm the lone virgin now since…since—"

"Since Ry *deflowered* me?" Carrie supplied, then snorted when Steph laughed. "Trust me…it's probably the word he would use. I think he's some closet Victorian morals cop or something."

"Are we talking about the same Ry Evans here?"

"Yeah, I know. Given his reputation with women, it's a little hard to figure, huh?"

Steph pushed away from the desk to snap a yellow leaf off a lush philodendron flourishing on the windowsill. Beyond the open blinds, the sky was already turning the gunmetal-gray shade that would deepen in a few more minutes to the black of evening. Night came early to West Texas in February.

"Maybe he's acting this way because it was you...and because you're special to him," Steph offered.

"Yeah. I'm special all right," Carrie said with a tired breath. So special he didn't have it in him to love her.

"So," Steph said, lowering her voice and eyeing Carrie with open curiosity from across the room, "was it, um, you know. The...sex. Oh, heck. *How* was it?"

How was it? Carrie let herself drift back to the night before and felt her bones melt at the memories.

"Incredible," she admitted as a surge of arousal that even her disappointment and anger couldn't quell, eddied through her.

Steph sighed dreamily, then jumped when a knock sounded on her office door. "Yes?" she said just as the door swung open—and Nathan Beldon walked in.

"Carrie," he said, relief filling his voice. "Thank God I finally found you."

Carrie drew her shoulders back, a defense against her pride, which had taken a hit from this man, too. "I don't think we have anything to say to each other, Nathan."

Nathan looked from Carrie to Stephanie, who was regarding him with barely veiled disdain. He flashed a smile that oozed charm and begged for understanding. "Would you mind leaving us alone for a few minutes? I realize it's a huge imposition, but I really need to discuss something with Carrie in private."

Stephanie looked toward Carrie for her reaction.

"It's okay, Steph," she said, deciding it would be best to just clear the air, throw him out on his ear and get on with her life. "Nathan and I have some unfinished business. It won't take but a few minutes."

"I'll be right outside in the other room," Steph said, looking uneasy and uncertain about the wisdom of leaving Carrie with Nathan.

"Let's make this easy, okay?" Carrie said to Nathan after Stephanie reluctantly left the room, shutting the door behind her. "You're not what I thought you were. You're not *who* I thought you were. And you are definitely not someone I care about having in my life. Beyond that, I really have nothing to say to you."

With that, she rose from behind Stephanie's desk and headed for the door.

"You're not going anywhere, you simpering little bitch."

Carrie was so stunned—by his words, by the rancor licking through them—she froze, certain her mind was playing tricks on her. But then she saw his face. Hatred. Stark and vivid.

Who *was* this person? And how could she ever

have thought he could become someone special to her?

Suddenly she was frightened. And the only place she wanted to be was gone. "Goodbye, Nathan."

"I said, you aren't going anywhere," Roman Birkenfeld snarled and grabbed the high-and-mighty Ms. Whelan's arm when she tried to walk past him.

Good, he thought, when her expression registered both pain and a shock so acute she couldn't even speak. He saw the thread of fear in her eyes. And he liked it. He hadn't planned on getting rough with her—at least not yet. He'd planned on making her see reason, win back her trust so he could use her to get to Natalie Perez and ultimately his money through Carrie's brother in a little more civilized manner. But he was beyond civilized now and her holier-than-thou attitude was the last straw.

"Take your hand off me."

"Let's get something straight. You're not giving the orders here. I am." He dug into his jacket pocket, pulled out the gun Jason Carter had procured for him. The surge of power he felt when she drew in a gasping breath was almost as good as sex. "Don't even think about screaming for help or running. You might get away but I promise you, your friend—Stephanie, is it?—she and anyone else within ten yards of you are as good as dead if you do. Are we clear?

"Are we clear?" he repeated, jerking hard on her

arm for good measure. He relished her wince of pain. The confusion clouding her face was almost comical.

"Yes," she whispered finally, and he could see she'd finally figured it out. He wasn't playing around here. "I won't scream. I…won't run."

"Because you know who will get hurt if you do."

"Yes. I know. Nathan…I don't understand. Why are you doing this?"

"My name is not Nathan. It's Roman Birkenfeld, and other than that, the only thing you need to know is that I've had it with this Podunk town, this situation and the fact that thanks to your future sister-in-law, everything in my life has turned to crap."

"Natalie? What does Nat…wait. B-Birkenfeld? But Roman Birkenfeld is the doctor who—"

"I know who I am," he growled, heard the barely controlled hysteria in his voice and forced himself to stop, compose himself. "You are all so gullible," he added, feeling another small power surge over that fact. He'd fooled them. He'd fooled them all into believing he was Beldon. He'd even fooled Beldon into believing he could trust him. He was superior to every one of these country bumpkins. But he was also as dead as he'd left Beldon if he didn't get his money.

The phone call he'd received last night was very thorough, detailing exactly what was going to happen to him if he didn't pay up within twenty-four hours. He had no idea how they'd found him, but the fact that they had was telling of the gravity of the threat.

Until a few minutes ago, he'd still been counting on Stokes and Carter to come through with the half mil Natalie had taken from him. But Tommy Stokes had just called. He and Carter had bungled the job of stealing his money back from the Cattleman's Club—bungled it so badly that Carter was in jail, and Stokes, after telling him to stick his grunt job where the sun don't shine, was headed for parts unknown.

That made Carrie Whelan his last resort. Big brother would come running with his money now if he wanted to see his sister alive again. Of course, he'd have to kill her now regardless, but Whelan didn't have to know that until it was too late.

"Let's go," he said, tucking the gun back into his jacket pocket, then positioning his body beside and a little behind her so he could prod the snub-nose barrel into her ribs. "Just follow my lead. If anyone asks, we decided to go have a cup of coffee and talk things out, got it?"

She nodded jerkily.

"Your friend's life depends on how convincing you are," he reminded her for good measure and pushed her toward the door.

He was insane. Carrie was certain of it as she sat on the floor in the corner of a room that was cold and damp and from the echoing hollowness of every sound, empty. She'd decided they were in a warehouse...or a garage. Maybe. She wasn't sure. Couldn't tell. Once Birkenfeld had gotten her into his car, he'd blindfolded her, then taped her hands together behind her back and driven.

Her questions had gotten her nowhere. He'd just ranted on and on to himself about getting his money, damning Natalie and her interference, swearing how he was going to make her pay. How he was going to make everyone pay.

Natalie's name was the only connection Carrie had been able to make. Natalie's and Roman Birkenfeld. And that was enough to tell the tale. She'd overheard Natalie and Travis talking. She knew that Birkenfeld was the doctor from Chicago who had tried to steal baby Autumn. What she didn't understand was how *she* fit in. Of course, considering that she was scared out of her ever-loving mind, there was a pretty good possibility she might have missed something. Something vital. Something that might save her life…and she had no doubt about it, her life was definitely on the line here.

She'd tried to concentrate on what he was saying…tried to connect with some semblance of time and distance, but the blindfold had skewed her perceptions. Adrenaline had ratcheted up her heartbeat. And fear had her mind reeling with possibilities too horrible to fathom.

Still, she tried to focus. As best as she could figure, they'd traveled for around twenty minutes before he'd finally stopped and dragged her out of his car. The hollow ring of the doors he slammed behind them as he'd led her through what felt like a labyrinth of halls and stairways made her think of cavernous spaces.

It had to be a warehouse, she finally decided. Abandoned, most likely, if the absence of heat was any clue. Yet...something...the smell...it was right there...but not quite. She knew that she knew what she was smelling...but like a bubble that burst just as you reached out and touched it, recognition kept eluding her.

"Get up," he ordered abruptly.

She did as he asked, using the wall at her back for leverage and balance since she couldn't see, couldn't use her hands to assist her.

"We're going to have a little chat with your brother. All you have to tell him is that you're all right and that he's to do what I ask or I'm going to kill you. Got it?"

Or I'm going to kill you. She got that part loud and clear.

She nodded, his cold-blooded words echoing in her mind as her heart jackhammered inside her chest.

"What's his cell phone number?"

She thought, swallowed. "I...I don't know. It's programmed into my cell phone but I don't remember the number."

She flinched when he swore.

"It's in my purse," she added hastily. "My phone. It's in my purse."

She heard things hit the floor as he rifled through what she assumed was her purse. "How do you access your phone book?'' he asked finally, and again she assumed he'd found her phone.

She had to think, really think about it, but finally remembered and told him. She heard the electronic beep of buttons being pushed, then waited, not knowing whether to breathe a sigh of relief or dread when it became apparent he made a connection with Trav.

At this point there was only one thing she did know. He had no intentions of letting her live. Whether Travis came for her or not, there wasn't a reason in the world compelling enough for Birkenfeld to keep her alive.

Oddly, it wasn't herself she was worried about as much as she was worried about Travis and Ry. They'd feel responsible. If something happened to her, they would feel responsible for the rest of their lives.

And she'd never once told Ry—knot-headed Victorian-minded throwback that he was—that she loved him. That realization finally galvanized her resolve. She decided she wasn't going to just cower like a frightened animal and let Birkenfeld kill her.

Animal. That was it! That was the odor milling under the scent of antiseptic and dust that she hadn't been able to place. My God. She knew where she was.

Trav was in his car, heading for a meeting at the club when his cell rang. He checked the digital read-out, saw it was Carrie's number. "Hey, bear, what's up?" he said cheerily when he answered.

"I've got something you want, Whelan."

Travis almost rear-ended the car in front of him. "Who is this?" he demanded, an uneasy punch of foreboding lurching through his blood stream.

"Roman Birkenfeld."

Unease gave way to panic. "Birkenfeld? What the hell are you—"

"Shut up," the man on the other end of the line demanded, giving Trav no choice but to obey. "Just listen. It's like I said. I've got something you want, and you've got something I want. I've got your sister."

"You son of a—"

"Yeah, yeah, you're one tough Texan, but I'm in control here. You want her back, you'll do exactly as I say. No questions. Do you understand?"

"I want to talk to her," Trav demanded, breaking out in a cold sweat.

He heard a muffled cry—of pain, of surprise—and it damn near ripped his heart out. And then he heard her voice. And the tremor in it undid him.

"Trav."

"Carrie. Oh, God, bear. What's he done to you?"

"N-nothing. Yet. I'm…I'm okay. I'm…I'm tough. Come from good…stock."

His heart clenched at her bravado. "Where are you, sweetie?"

"I…Nathan…I mean, Roman…he blindfolded

me. Trav...I love you. Always...remember Fort Worth—''

Birkenfeld yanked the phone from her from her hand. ''This is all very touching,'' he broke in, cutting her off, ''but now we've got business, Whelan. And so you know...she's dead or as good as if you don't follow my instructions to the letter.''

''You put so much as a bruise on her—''

''You are not in a position to be issuing ultimatums!'' Birkenfeld yelled, sounding on the edge and on the brink of toppling over. ''One more word and you will never see her alive again.''

Trav bit his tongue and swore that he'd rip the bastard limb from limb when he found him. *If* he found him. Until he did, he had little choice but to play Birkenfeld's game.

''Better,'' Birkenfeld said. ''Now, this is what's going to happen.''

Nine

Ry had felt helpless before. When you were flat on your back on a rodeo arena floor, waiting out your fate as a thousand pounds of pissed-off bronc bucked and rolled above you and one hoof strike could end your career—or worse, your life—you were on intimate terms with helpless. On one or two dicey TCC missions, when he'd been caught in a wait-and-see situation while his brain screamed for decisive action, he'd understood the power of that seemingly benign word.

But he'd never breathed helplessness, tasted it, lived it like he had in the moments since Travis had called together him and the two other TCC members involved in Natalie's case and broken the worst possible news.

Roman Birkenfeld, the man they'd all thought was Nathan Beldon, the man who had tried to kill Natalie and steal her baby, was holding Carrie hostage.

Carrie. The little girl he'd watched grow into a beautiful woman. The woman he'd wanted and tried to keep away from. The woman he'd finally made incredible love with. The woman he just might damn well *be* in love with.

"Go over it again," he demanded of Trav as he, Alex Kent and Darin ibn Shakir gathered, grim-faced around a conference table in a private meeting room in the back of the club. "There's got to be something…something we're missing, damn it, that will lead us to her."

Darin exchanged a look with Alex that relayed what all four men were thinking. Birkenfeld had lost it. He'd kidnapped Carrie and then contacted Travis, demanding Travis deliver the half million in cash the men had recovered the night Natalie and baby Autumn had literally fallen into their arms at the Royal Diner. He wanted the money in exchange for Carrie's life. Trav was waiting for a call back from Birkenfeld that would tell him when and where to leave the money.

"The bastard has a real penchant for trading in human lives," Darin said aloud.

Alex worked a hand over his jaw, his brows drawn tight. "Someone who steals and sells babies is about as warped as it gets."

"He has no intention of letting Carrie go," Darin

pointed out grimly as he looked from Travis to Ryan. "You understand that, don't you?"

All too well, Ry thought as he rose from the table to pace the room, out of his mind with rage and concern and drowning in that damnable sense of helplessness. "Tell me again exactly what she said," he demanded of Trav.

Trav drew a deep breath, closed his eyes and concentrated. "She said he'd blindfolded her. That she didn't know where she was. She said...she said, Trav...I love you." He had to stop, as emotion lodged in his throat, choking him. "And then she said something...something about...remember Fort Worth."

"Fort Worth?" Ry planted his hands on the table in front of Trav, leaned in close. "She was trying to tell you something. Does it mean anything to you?"

Trav shook his head, baffled. "Vacations. We sometimes took family vacations in Fort Worth. But that's too obvious. Besides, he couldn't have taken her that far...not this soon. When I talked to Stephanie, she said they left the library together a little over an hour ago."

Ry pushed away from the table, paced the room.

"So what did you do on your vacations?" Alex asked, prodding further for some clue that would help locate Carrie before it was too late.

"Mostly, we went to the stock shows. Wait," Trav said, stopping abruptly. "I remember something else now...when I asked her if she was okay, she said she was tough…something about coming from good stock.''

"Fort Worth—stock show. Good stock. *Stock*.'' Ry mulled the information around in his head. Then he swore and headed for the door. ''She handed it to us on a platter. He's got her at the abandoned stock-yards on the edge of town.''

Alex caught up with Ry, grabbed his arm, then released it immediately when he saw the deadly intent in his friend's eyes. ''Look, man. You can't head out there half-cocked. You don't even know for certain if that's where he's holding her.''

''I don't know she's not there, either.'' He looked over his shoulder at Trav. ''When Birkenfeld calls again to set up the exchange, stall him so he'll stay put. And if you come up with a different location, call my cell. Leave Vincente out of it for now. I don't want the Royal PD barreling in there with sirens screaming and spooking Birkenfeld into doing something really stupid.''

''Ry—'' Darin tried one last time but Ryan was already out the door.

The three men exchanged concerned looks, but none of them tried to stop him. If he was right, he might be Carrie's best shot at getting out of this in one piece. If he was wrong—then they were back at square one and Carrie's life might not be worth the phony birth certificates Birkenfeld issued for the babies he'd stolen.

"I'll get ahold of David and Clint and have them standing by," Alex said, pulling out his cell.

Darin rested a hand on Trav's shoulder. "Now we wait."

"Yeah," Trav echoed, staring bleakly at his cell phone, willing it to ring. "Now we wait."

Carrie sat huddled on the floor. She was cold. Her butt hurt. So did her knees from when Nathan...rather, Roman Birkenfeld had pushed her down on the rough concrete. Minutes, hours...or it could have been days that had passed since he'd placed the first call to her brother demanding money and then the second call to set up an exchange location.

The part of her that had remained focused knew it had been less than an hour since he'd brought her here. Less than fifteen minutes since he'd hung up from talking to Trav a second time and arranging to make the exchange. The part of her that had always been pragmatic also knew it might be her last hour. Birkenfeld was crazy.

Between calls he'd ranted and raved even more about how Natalie was going to pay for ruining his nice, orderly little business. And how Travis would never see his child again when he was through. He'd even brought Ry into his lunatic ramblings, vowing to kill him for humiliating him.

She had no illusion that she was also on his short list of murder candidates.

And she had to do something…soon. She was still blindfolded, but oddly, her loss of sight had turned into an advantage. Her other senses were keener. Like her sense of smell that had helped her figure out what that odd mixture of antiseptic, leather, cow manure and whitewash was. Now, if only Trav had picked up on her stockyard clues when she'd spoken with him.

She could also hear things now she wouldn't normally hear. Birkenfeld was rooting about in her purse again, like a squirrel digging for nuts. He evidently found the emergency candy bar she always carried because she heard the tear of paper and the sounds of him chowing down. Creep.

Then she heard something else…just the tiniest inkling of a sound…and immediately started talking to cover what she prayed were stealthy footsteps approaching the door.

"I have to go to the bathroom," she said in a loud, desperate voice.

"And you think I give a fig?" Birkenfeld actually snorted out a laugh. "In about two minutes it won't matter what you have to do."

"You're going to kill me, aren't you?"

"It's not that difficult, you know. Taking a life."

Oh, God. Carrie swallowed and forced herself to keep him talking. "You've already killed someone?"

"It won't go as easy for you as it did for Nathan Beldon," he said, answering her question without actually addressing it. "Sadly, sweet Carrie, I'm fresh out of pharmaceuticals so I can't just give you a little injection and send you off to never-never land. No, it's going to be a little messier for you. Unfortunately, that makes it messier for me, too."

"It…doesn't have to be this way, you know," she said, swallowing back her terror. "We have money. Much more than a half a million dollars. My brother is loaded. And I've got a trust fund that will make your stolen money look like loose change."

"I didn't steal that money," he shouted, infuriated suddenly. "I earned it…not legally, of course. Certainly not ethically, but finding babies for willing buyers takes a certain amount of finesse and skill."

"I repeat," she said, swallowing back bile, "you can get much more in ransom from my brother if you will actually let me go."

She heard the unmistakable sound of an ammunition clip sliding home.

"I'm really a little sorry about this," he said, and she heard him walk toward her, his breathing heavy. "But…what must be done, must be—"

A loud crash split the air like a freight train. The unmistakable crack and snap of wood shattering…like a table breaking followed, then the thudding grunt of fist hitting flesh. A shot rang out.

Carrie screamed and pulled herself into a tight little ball, shielding her head with her hands, not knowing what might come flying at her—knowing only that she and Birkenfeld were no longer alone and if there was a God, it was the cavalry who had arrived just in the nick of time.

She didn't know how much time passed as a struggle raged around her. Something hit her arm, and she curled tighter into herself, her heart beating so loud it drowned out any other sound.

Her world was reduced to a tight knot of fear…when a pair of strong hands cupped her shoulders.

She flinched and tried to skitter away.

"Baby…it's okay. It's Ry. I've got you."

Gentle hands worked at the knot on the blindfold then pulled it away from her face with tender care.

It was dark, both inside and outside the room that appeared to have once been a storage area of sorts. Her vision was blurry—from the pressure of the cloth, from tears of terror—but she finally put it all together and recognized the voice, recognized the scent and the strength of the man who pulled her carefully to her feet and into his arms.

"Ry." She threw her arms around his neck.

"I know, baby. I know. It's over. That son of a bitch is never going to get his hands on you again."

She clung to him, felt moisture wet her cheeks and Ry's shirt where she pressed her face into his chest. From the corner of her eyes, she saw Birkenfeld in a crumpled heap by the door.

"He…he wa-was going to sh-shoot me."

Ry's strong arms folded tighter around her, pressed her face against his neck, holding her together while adrenaline kicked into high gear and she started shaking uncontrollably.

"Not on my watch, sweet pea," he murmured into the top of her head, but his voice was shaking, too, as he rocked her. "Not on my watch."

In the distance she heard sirens, then the squeal of tires...and the unmistakable sound of feet scrabbling over concrete.

Ry looked over his shoulder, then abruptly let her go. She followed his gaze to see Birkenfeld had come around and was crawling toward the door that hung by a broken hinge.

"You can't run far enough fast enough," Ry growled, grabbing him by the back of his shirt and hauling him to his feet.

That's when Birkenfeld proved he was not only crazy, he was stupid. He took a wild swing...it was all the invitation Ry needed to lay the hammer down.

He cocked his arm back and punched him in the breadbasket. When Birkenfeld doubled over with an oophing groan, Ry followed with a hard uppercut to his jaw. Birkenfeld stumbled back against the wall with a whimper...and Ry went in for the kill.

"That's for touching her, you sick bastard." He slammed his fist into his face. "And this is for hurting her." Another head-snapping jab to his jaw. "And this is for scaring her."

Trav came racing into the room, took one look at Carrie and scooped her into his arms. Alex and Darin skidded in on his heels...and had the regrettable task of pulling Ry off Birkenfeld before he beat him to a bloody pulp.

"Easy, big guy," Alex said, holding Ry back by his left arm, while Darin got a death grip on his right.

"Save something for the uniforms to haul to jail," Darin suggested.

Both men relaxed marginally when Ry seemed to realize he'd gone a little crazy himself.

"I'm good," he said, shaking free of their hold and wiping a swollen knuckle over his jaw. "I'm good," he repeated and, forcing a deep breath, made himself back off just as Chief Vincente and his men arrived, guns drawn.

"Nice y'all could make the party," Ry said, settling himself down.

"Yeah, well, we came as soon as you called to confirm you spotted this cretin's car," Alex said with a grin. "Besides...we wanted to give you time to play hero."

"You're not going to be able to pin anything on me," Birkenfeld whined from his slumped position on the floor. Through bruised and swollen eyes and bloody lips, he glared first at Ry then at Darin. "I'll sue for assault and battery. I'll be out of jail in twenty-four hours. And then we'll see how you *heroes* feel."

"Can we say *delusional,* boys and girls?" Alex added with a grunt of disgust. "Get him out of here, Vincente."

"Why don't I just help you boys out and get him

into your cruiser?'' Ry suggested to the two officers who had followed their police chief into the room.

''Oh, I think your work is done here, Ry,'' Alex observed. ''I'll do the honors. Besides, something— or someone—else needs your attention.''

Darin hauled Birkenfeld roughly to his feet and shoved him in the general direction of the officers and the door. ''Let's go. Your fun is just beginning.''

Ry turned back to Carrie, snuggled and shaking in Trav's arms. Something inside him knotted, hardened and he wished with everything in him that he had one more shot at Birkenfeld.

Bloodlust. He'd never known exactly what it had meant to feel it.

He knew it now.

He'd wanted Birkenfeld's blood for what he'd done to Carrie. Still had a lingering taste for it as he walked across the room, wanting to take her back in his arms so badly, he shook with it.

''Need to have a word with you, Evans.''

Ry stopped at the sound of Wayne Vincente's voice.

Eyes on Carrie, he let out a resolved breath. ''Sure. What do you need to know, Chief?''

Vincente pulled out a notebook. ''Why don't you just start at the top and we'll see how it goes from there.

''Now, wait up there, son. I'll have to interview Carrie, too,'' Wayne added when Trav, sheltering

Carrie under his arm, started walking her toward the door.

"Tomorrow," Ry and Trav said in unison, neither man willing to make her go through any more than she'd already been through today.

"I'm taking her home," Trav informed the chief, who recognized the bald determination in Trav's eyes and finally gave a reluctant nod.

"I'll stop by in the morning then, Carrie, if that's okay with you."

"That will be fine," she said, gathering the courage Ry had been aching to see since he'd found her huddled and terrified on the floor.

A long hour later, Stephanie opened Carrie's door at Ry's knock. He stood just inside the foyer for a long moment when he spotted Carrie on the sofa. She looked bruised, he thought, and for a suspended moment he considered charging right back out the door, finding Birkenfeld's jail cell and finishing the job of rearranging the sick bastard's face.

For Carrie's sake he settled himself, got his rage under control. For the next several moments all he could do was look at her.

She was wrapped from head to toe in a soft pink robe. Her hair was wet—as though she'd just gotten out of the shower. Trav sat beside her like a ham-fisted mother hen. A man of decisiveness and confidence, Trav currently looked powerless and concerned and as if he'd rip the head off anyone who so much as breathed a word that might upset his baby sister.

Only, she wasn't a baby, Ry thought as his gaze roamed over the soft curves beneath her robe. She was a woman. A woman whose body he knew intimately. A woman who had been through more than any woman should have to endure.

The hands she'd wrapped around a heavy pottery mug to warm them were no longer shaking, he noticed with a small measure of relief. And when she sipped, then lowered the mug, and a delicate and adorable chocolate-colored mustache lined her upper lip, something inside his chest melted like a sun-warmed ice flow.

"How's she doing?" he asked as Stephanie took his jacket and hung it on the oak-and-brass hall tree.

"She's tougher than she looks," Steph said softly. "She was a little shocky when I got here, but she's doing better now. Better than Trav, if you want to know the truth," she added with a sympathetic smile.

"He call you to come over?"

"From his cell on their way home."

He squeezed her arm. "You're a good friend."

"Not good enough, or I never would have let her leave the library with that creep."

"Hey, you can't think that way. You couldn't have known. Hell, none of us did."

She let out a deep breath. "And that's the real scary part, isn't it? You just never know."

No, he agreed, you just never knew.

He drew another settling breath as a vivid image of Carrie, bound and blindfolded and huddling on the floor like a child, flashed front and center. It was good, he decided, that he hadn't been able to get to her before now. Now he was at least a little calmer. She needed calm from him, not the kind of fractured control he'd been working to get under wraps on the drive from the stockyard.

He'd patiently answered all of Vincente's questions, watched in grim silence as Alex and Darin had helped the two police officers "escort" a handcuffed Birkenfeld out of the building then deposit him "gently" into the back seat of the black-and-white. Birkenfeld had whined and complained and hurled threats about getting even with all of them. And all the while all Ry had wanted to do was get to Carrie.

Now he was here. And now, he was finally able to take a good long look at the woman he loved to make sure she was all right.

The woman he loved. Yeah. He loved her. He suspected he'd loved her for years—and he was angry as hell with himself that it took almost losing her to bring him to terms with the truth. Hopefully it wasn't too late to convince her she loved him, too.

Jaw set in determination, he walked into the living room. Her head came up when she heard his footsteps on the polished oak floor.

"Hey, bear," he said gently. Crouching down in front of her, he covered her knees with his hands.

Her eyes were big and round and still just a little

wild. But she smiled for him. Yes, it was forced, but it was a smile and it told him she was rallying…like she always rallied when life kicked her in the teeth and set her on her tail.

"Hey, Rambo," she said, and he let out a breath that had been backed up in his lungs since he'd found out Birkenfeld had abducted her. "Remind me to never make you mad, okay?"

"Oh…you think I was mad back there?" He squeezed her thighs, smiled then found he had a hell of a time holding on to it when all he wanted to do was drag her into his arms and hold her. "Nah. I was just expressing an opinion."

She looked down at his hands, touched a finger to his scraped knuckles. "Thank you," she whispered. Tears filled her eyes. She laughed shakily and blinked them back. "Sorry. I have *definitely* surpassed my quota in the waterworks department today."

His gaze sliced to Trav who was watching Ry with a hard-edged glare that could have meant anything from "I'd like to kill that bastard Birkenfeld" to "I hate to see her hurting like this" to "Get your bear paws off my sister, pal."

Ry didn't care what Trav's look meant. He kept his hands where they were…and his gaze fixed on Carrie's face. "I want to talk to your sister, Trav. Alone."

He loved this woman. Cared about her the way he'd never cared about anyone else. And whether

Trav liked it or not, whether it cost him their friendship, he was going to do everything in his power to convince Carrie she needed him in her life. Starting right now.

"And what if I don't want to leave her alone with you?"

At the grim sound of Trav's voice, Ry looked up and into a pair of brown eyes set with stubborn determination. He closed his eyes, let out a breath. So, they were going to do this the hard way.

He stood—so did Trav. And, expressions hard, they faced off against each other.

"What I have to say to Carrie is between the two of us."

Trav gave him a slant-eyed stare. "What could you possibly have to say to my sister that you couldn't say in front of me?"

Ry studied the face of the man he regarded as a brother. And knew he was going to miss him.

"Okay...look. I never meant for this to happen but it has. I fought it. But I lost. So here it is. I love your sister, Trav. I love her.

"So...if you want to have it out with me right here and now then I guess we'll just have to have it out. You can whale on me all you want." He held his arms out at his sides, his stance a study in supplication. "Have at it. But I won't hit you back. You can beat me into the ground if you think I deserve it—and I probably do. Lord knows I've beat myself up about it often enough—but I'm going to have Carrie for my own, one way or another, with or without your approval.''

Speech ended, he watched Trav's face and braced for the first blow.

''Well,'' Trav finally said, then surprised the hell out of Ry when he broke into a broad grin. ''It's about damn time you slow-witted lug nut. I've been waiting for *years* for you to come to your senses and realize you love her.''

Ry blinked, dumfounded. ''Say what?''

''Take her,'' Trav said with a laugh. ''With my blessings. She's yours. Now maybe the two of you will lose those lost-puppy looks every time you see each other, and get on with your lives.''

Trav stuck out his hand. After a moment's hesitation while Trav's reaction set in, Ry took it. Shook it hard, then covered it with his other hand and shook some more.

''You knew?'' he asked, incredulous.

Trav snorted then rolled his eyes at Steph who was smiling—a bit tearfully—in the background. ''Yeah. The whole damn town knew…everyone, that is, except you two.''

Grinning from ear to ear with relief and elation, Ry turned to Carrie.

His smile fell like a hot air balloon with a burst seam.

Oh-oh. She was mad. Nest-of-hornets mad.

''Carrie?'' he asked, reaching for her as she rose from the sofa.

She batted his hand away. "You're going to *have* me?" she spit out. "*Have* me?"

"Oh, bear. Sweetheart. That's not—"

"And you." She ignored Ry and rounded on her brother. "You're *giving* me to him? You *give* me to him and then shake on the deal like...like I'm some piece of property you can pass around as you see fit?"

She shoved her fists deep into the pockets of her pink robe—then just as fast, jerked them out again and crossed them over her breasts. "Well, you can both go straight to the devil. Nobody *gives* me to anybody. And nobody *has* me unless I want to be had.

"Go away. Both of you. Before I decide to express my *opinion* of your XY-chromosomes mentality and your incurable macho thought processes by breaking a couple very expensive vases over your very thick, very dense skulls."

"Whoa-ho," Trav said, looking marginally chastised and wholly entertained. "Looks like you're in for a knock-down, drag-out—"

"Save it," Ryan interrupted, his grin turning into a steely glare. "You heard the lady. She wants you to leave."

"I want you *both* to leave," Carrie reminded him, and with only a little imagination Ry could picture smoke rolling out of her ears.

"Steph," Ry said politely, "could I bother you to make sure Trav finds the door?"

Stephanie threw Carrie an apologetic smile then snagged Trav's arm. "Come on, Travis. I think they want to be alone. Well…at least one of them does."

"Bye, Steph. Get lost, Whelan," Ry said, following them to the door and shoving Trav's coat into his chest.

"My money's on you, bud," Trav managed to say just as Ry shut the door on Trav's stupid grin and Steph's whispered wish for good luck.

He stared at the closed door for a moment, gathering his thoughts. He was going to need luck. Lots of it.

He'd blown it, big-time. Twice. Once yesterday morning when he hadn't told Carrie what she needed to hear…and just now when he'd said the words but managed to make them sound like a business transaction instead of over-his-head-crazy-till-he-hurt in love with her.

He winced, remembering how badly he'd handled things. She'd wanted morning-after kisses and "I love you." She'd deserved both. And he'd been so quaking in his boots scared of everything he'd been feeling, he'd given her stone cold looks and "We need to get married." And just now—well, just now he'd been a big dumb jerk.

On a deep breath he threw the dead bolt. Mouth set in determination he turned, then leaned back against the door and settled in for a standoff. Something told him it might be a long one.

Ten

"**I** have been kidnapped, blindfolded and bound hand and foot. I've been held hostage, roughed up and was certain I was going to die," Carrie said, narrowing her eyes at the man who leaned back against her closed door like some dark angel who had settled in for the duration or judgment day, whichever came first.

"All in all, it's been a pretty full day," she added as her anger built. "And now I'm tired. And I'm cranky. And I may very well be just a tad dangerous, Evans, so if I were you, I'd waltz on out that door and take your testosterone-induced attitude with you."

He compressed his lips, stared at her through narrowed eyes and finally shook his head. "No can do, bear. I'm not leaving you. Not until we've had a chance to talk this out."

"You've already done enough talking, if you ask me."

"Too much talking and not nearly enough asking," he agreed. "I'm asking now, bear. Will you marry me?"

She didn't want it to, but her heart kicked her—hard—right beneath her sternum and reminded her how much she loved this man.

She didn't want to love him right now. She wanted to be mad at him. She *needed* to be mad at him and his nerve that made him think he could just dance back into her life and tell her he loved her and figure that meant he was entitled to *have* her.

And darn it, it felt good to feel something other than fear. It felt good to be mad, and she wanted to ride on the wave for a little while yet. Make *him* sweat. Make *him* wonder.

"I'm not sure I want to marry you," she announced with her arms crossed over her chest and her chin cocked. "Even if it turns out I'm pregnant. I told you. You're not obligated to anything."

Very slowly he pushed away from the door and, like a big, sleek cat stalking his prey, prowled slowly toward her. "How about I tell you what I *am* obligated to?"

The look in his eyes was dark and dangerous...and so hot she felt the burn all the way to her toes.

"I'm obligated to this love I feel for you. This love that's so strong it's eating me up inside with wanting you and needing you and trying to figure out how I can fix the botched-up mess I've made of things between us."

Oh, God. No fair. How did a woman stay mad in the face of such wonderful, achingly loving words? And how badly did she really want to stay mad, she wondered as he moved directly in front of her, cupped her upper arms in his big hands and pulled her slowly toward him.

"I'm obligated to make you understand that I have loved you forever but I just didn't know what to do about it...what to do with all these feelings I've tried to fight and tried to hide and tried to tell myself were wrong."

Tears welled in her eyes while her heart swelled with love. "Wrong? How can love be wrong?"

"It can't be. But us lug-nut types don't often see the truth." He smiled then and what was left of her resolve crumbled like dust in a dry riverbed.

"You've had a crush on me for a long time, bear. I knew that. I also figured it was just a little hero worship and it would eventually go away...and then you'd go away, too, and find the guy you really loved. Really needed to make you happy."

"You are a lug nut, you big dope. What I really need is you...what I've always needed was you."

He closed his eyes, let out a breath that felt wonderfully like relief as it feathered across her face.

"God, I hope so. Carrie—" he paused, searched her face then went down on one knee "—I'm going to do this right this time."

He took both of her hands in his, pressed his lips to her knuckles. "I love you. I will always love you. Will you make me the happiest man on the face of the earth and do me the honor of becoming my wife? Will you have me? Hold me? In sickness and in health. For richer—"

Her happy laughter cut him off. "Hey...I think you'd better save some for the ceremony."

He looked up and met her gaze, and she could swear she saw tears swimming in those beautiful brown eyes. "Is that a yes?"

She turned her hands in his until she could grip his fingers as hard as he was gripping hers. "That's an absolutely, positively yes, I'll marry you, Ryan."

He released her hands, wrapped his arms around her hips and pressed his face against her belly. "I'll never make you sorry," he promised, pressing a kiss there. "I love you so much."

A choked sob burst out as she threaded her fingers through his hair. "You'd better," she said, and laughed as he rose to his feet and kissed her. "Because I'm not letting you back out of this, Evans. It's a done deal, got it?"

"Not yet it's not," he said, "We're going to seal this with a little more than a kiss."

Scooping her into his arms, Ry carried her into the bedroom.

"You are everything to me," he whispered, setting her on her feet beside the bed.

He reached for the belt holding her robe together. His hands were trembling as he parted the soft chenille and found her fragrant and naked beneath it.

Swallowing thickly, he watched it slip from her shoulders and pool in a cloud of pink on the floor at her feet.

He spanned her narrow waist with widespread fingers. "God. You're so beautiful."

"Make me feel alive," she whispered and, lying back on the bed, tugged him down with her. "Make me forget about what almost happened today."

Her voice broke with emotion, and in that moment he'd have done anything...anything to make her forget about how close she'd come to death. He wanted her thinking only of him and of her and the life they would have together.

His breath stalled on a harsh intake of air when she reached for him, frantically worked the snap then the zipper on his jeans as he roughly undid his shirt buttons and shrugged out of it. He groaned when she reached inside his pants and cupped him, then swore viciously when he had to pull away and tug off his boots before he could get out of his jeans and socks.

But then it was skin on skin, heartbeat to heartbeat...and her wild and urgent need that stole his breath, robbed his sanity.

"Please, please, please," she begged, raking her

nails along his back and opening her thighs to welcome him inside her.

He couldn't hold back. Her hunger fed his. He touched her there, found her wet and swollen and so ready he lost his ability to finesse, lost his intentions to soothe and found in her a fierce need that demanded he answer…and answer now.

He guided himself to her opening, felt her clench like hot wax around him and plunged deep. She cried out and clung to him. With her arms, her legs, her mouth, she wrapped herself around him and demanded with urgent whispers and wanton pleas to give her everything, to take everything, to be everything. Everything good. Everything right. Everything that mattered.

He hesitated only a moment…a moment in which he feared he might hurt her. But the moment streaked by on a blaze of burning desire when she lifted her hips and locked her ankles around his waist, rising to his deep thrust like steam rising in the morning mist. Like smoke drifting from a red-hot fire. Like life, surging from near death in celebration.

And then there was nothing but her. The silk of her skin, the scent of her desire, the heat of her body that welcomed him like dawn welcomes the sun. He sank into her, became one with her, became life for her with all the passion and glory the act of love had intended.

And when he felt her body clench and shudder and tasted her soft cry of release against his lips, he pumped one last time and went the same way she had...spilling all the love he'd held in check for the woman who owned him heart and soul.

She was snuggled against his side, her long leg draped over his thighs, her arm wrapped around his waist. Ry could feel the even cadence of her breath against his throat, feel her heartbeat pulse in a steady, resting rhythm against his ribs. Nothing, he decided, could feel as good as Carrie.

Weary and spent, he reached up to gently tug a strand of red hair from the corner of his mouth.

"I'm sorry," he whispered when she stirred, then stretched. "I didn't mean to wake you."

"You didn't. I wasn't asleep. I was just lying here, thinking how lucky I am."

He felt himself tense all over. "He never should have gotten his hands on you."

"I wasn't thinking about Birkenfeld. I was thinking about you." She hugged him hard, pressed a kiss to his throat. "You are a wonderful lover."

He grunted. "So you like it rough, do you?"

"I like it with you. Rough. Tender. Slow. Sweet. Anytime. Any way."

"I didn't hurt you?"

He felt her smile against his skin. "I was sort of worried that *I'd* hurt you. You'd better let me see your back."

She was referring to her fingernails. "I'm fine. I'm more than fine," he added, and turned to his side so he could see her face. "I'm sorry I've been so slow on the uptake."

When she touched her fingertips to his lips, he sucked them inside and bit lightly. "We'll think of ways for you to make it up to me."

He was about to suggest a particular way for him to do just that when her phone rang.

"Go ahead," she said when he lifted a brow.

He snagged it on the second ring. "Yeah."

"Ry?" It was Trav.

"What's up?"

"How's Carrie?"

"She's fine," he said, then added with a smile. "She's great. In fact, how would you and Natalie feel about a double wedding?"

When Trav didn't respond, the hair on the back of his neck stood at attention. He sat up abruptly. "What? What's happened now?"

On the other end of the line, Trav exhaled a heavy breath. "Birkenfeld escaped."

Roman Birkenfeld slumped back in the cab of the semi and pretended he was asleep. That way he didn't have to answer the incessant questions of the beer-bellied, chain-smoking trucker who had picked him up a little over an hour ago. Besides, it hurt to talk.

That bastard Evans had made ground beef out of his lip. And those other two—one he'd heard the cops call Alex and the dark one with the goatee,

Darin something—they'd gotten in some sucker punches, too, when they'd shoved him into the cop car. Well, they'd also sealed their fate. He'd see them all dead before this was over. And it was far from over.

They'd actually thought they could arrest him, then send a rookie cop to transport him from the city to the county jail? He still couldn't believe how easy it had been. Still enjoyed thinking about the shocked look in the kid's eyes when the young cop realized his holster was empty.

"Yeah, that's right, Officer Smith," he'd taunted from the back seat of the police cruiser as he'd pressed the barrel just behind the rookie's left ear. "This is your gun, sonny…and as soon as you pull into that alley over there, you're going to unlock these cuffs if you want to live long enough to know what it feels like to shave something other than peach fuzz from that baby face of yours."

He'd pulled back the hammer and shoved the barrel tighter against the kid's skull. "No heroics. I don't want to kill a cop, but make no mistake, I will if you give me any trouble. Now, pull over and we'll just take care of getting me out of your hair."

That had been three hours ago. He smiled again, then winced when his lip reminded him of the beating he'd taken. The kid had just cashed his first paycheck as one of Royal's finest. Another nice stroke of luck. After parking the cruiser in a back alley, handcuffing the rookie in the back seat and giving him a crack on the head guaranteed to keep him out for a few hours, he'd made his way to a main highway.

And now he was just hours from Vegas. The half million was out of reach—at least for now—but he didn't need that money. Hell no. He could make his own money. All he needed was one good night at the tables and he'd be back in the chips. One good night and he could win enough money to pay off the loan sharks and start up another black-market baby ring.

One good night. That's all he needed. And once he got the monkey off his back, he'd attend to some unfinished business in Texas. He'd make those Texans pay for what they'd done to him. He'd make them all pay—starting with Natalie Perez and ending with those puffed-up play warriors who stood between him and his money.

He settled deeper into the seat, trying to get comfortable as the diesel rolled bumpily over the highway. He gave only a fleeting thought to Marci. If she knew what was good for her, she'd do what he'd told her to and disappear. He didn't need her anymore, but because she'd been a good time he hadn't killed her. She'd wish he had, however, if he ever found out she sold him out.

"How's Smith?" Ry asked the next day as he met with Trav, Alex, David, Darin and Clint in one of the club's meeting rooms.

"Slight concussion," Trav said with a scowl. "He'll be okay."

"I still don't understand." Darin's face was as dark as Trav's. "Why did they let a rookie transport Birkenfeld to county...and why alone?"

"I believe it's called budget cuts," Alex put in. "The police department is short-staffed, and Smith's partner checked out early with a bad case of stomach flu."

"Damn luck," said David Sorenson, who had been in this up to his elbows from the beginning, just like the rest of them.

"Dumb luck for Birkenfeld," Clint Andover agreed and let out a disgusted breath. "So now what?"

"Now I think someone should have a talk with Birkenfeld's nurse. If they can find her. She's bound to know something," Ry said. "Probably more than Jason Carter."

"Oh, yeah. Birkenfeld's hired muscle...the guy we caught trying to break into the club." Alex rubbed an index finger over his upper lip. "He had a lot to say, if I recall."

Ry nodded. "Yeah, he told Vincente that he figured Birkenfeld was headed for Vegas. Seems he's got a major-league gambling problem...so bad, in fact, he got into it with some Atlantic City loan sharks who are leaning on him real heavy to pay them off. According to Carter, Birkenfeld started his black-market baby ring to pay off those debts."

"And almost cost me Natalie and the baby. And Carrie," Trav added, his face paling.

Ry stared at his friend as a sick knot of anxiety over what had almost happened to these very special women curled in his gut. "We have to get him. No option."

Alex exchanged a look with Darin. "We will. Make no mistake. We will."

She wore nothing but lace. Little bits of it. Black and sheer. And she sat in the middle of her bed like a redheaded vixen, and all Ry could think was that he wanted it off.

"You are killing me, here," he said with a groan as he stood in Carrie's bedroom doorway and started working the buttons on his shirt.

She'd developed a penchant for driving him crazy over the past few days. He had it on good authority—hers—that she stayed awake nights figuring out ways to take him from zero to one hundred on the horny scale in less than ten seconds.

"Really? Truly?" She gave a roll of her shoulder and one thin, black strap fell down her arm, revealing the creamy fullness of her left breast. "You're not just saying that to make me feel good?"

"Keep it up," he warned, his breath catching at the sight of her coming to her knees and giving a tug at the string on her left hip that held her itsy-bitsy, teeny-weeny French bikini panties together. "Just keep it up and see what kind of trouble you get into."

"My middle name," she said, dimpling as the wisp of black lace that was her panties fell to the bed at her knees.

He groaned, then swore as he scrambled to toe off his boots and shuck his jeans. "You are a shameless little tease."

"Yeah. And you love it."

"I love you," he growled and, planting one knee on the mattress, reached for her.

"Again," she whispered against his lips as she threw her arms around his neck and leaned into him.

"I love you." He wrapped an arm around the back of her thighs, lifted and laid her none too gently on her back.

"Again," she demanded as he fell on top of her and pushed a leg between her thighs.

"You wanna talk or do you want to make love?" His fingers found her heat, expertly stroked.

This time, she was the one to moan. "We can talk later," she said breathlessly.

"Thought so," he managed to utter on a groan as he pushed up and into the sweetest heat and the most incredible sensation of coming home.

"So, you think there's a chance of finding him?" Carrie asked, her breath whispering across Ry's chest.

They'd made love for hours and now they lay in each other's arms, more pressing business on their minds.

"We'll find him. Alex and Darin will pretty much take over from here, but we'll all keep on top of the situation."

"Alex," she said aloud, as if she were pondering some huge dilemma.

"What about Alex?"

"Don't you think he and Stephanie would make a great couple?"

"Sweetie, I think Alex has a little more on his mind these days than couplehood."

"Yeah, I know. But still, I think it would be wonderful if those two could get together."

"Well, we really don't have much to say on the matter, do we?"

"I know. But Steph is so special…and Alex, he's such a hunk—"

"Hey," he said, sounding put out.

She leaned up on an elbow and kissed him. "Not as hunky as you of course."

"Much better," he said with a grin.

"Do you want babies, Ry?"

He was quiet for a minute. "Sweetie, I didn't even know I wanted to get married until a few days ago. But, yeah. Thinking about making a cute little red-headed hellion with you…well…I'd love to have a baby."

She kissed him again. "If we get busy on that right away, he or she will be almost the same age as his or her cousin."

"Umm...you want to run that by me again? What cousin?"

"Nat and Trav's baby."

"You mean Autumn?"

"I mean the baby Natalie is going to have around September."

He blinked, then tucked his chin to look down on her. "Natalie's pregnant?"

"Yeah. Isn't that great?"

"Your brother is a man of action."

"Oh, I seem to recall a little action coming from your side of the bed. Wanna put that in motion again?"

He laughed. "You've taken to this sex business in a big way, huh, bear?"

"Just making up for lost time," she whispered, and slid on top of him, straddling his hips with her thighs. "Just making up for lost time."

He knotted a hand in her hair, pushed her mouth down to his. "I was a fool to stay away from you for so long. I love you, Carrie."

"I know, baby. And don't worry. I'm never going to let you forget it."

He did forget his name for a while, though...when she took him in, took him deep and took him to that place where she was the only thing that mattered, the only thing that was...the only thing he would ever need.

*   *   *   *   *

Watch for the next installment of the
TEXAS CATTLEMAN'S CLUB:
THE STOLEN BABY

*Meet Alexander Kent—irredeemable
playboy, ladies' man and* husband? *His
undercover sting operation required a
wife, and prim librarian Stephanie Firth
was perfect for the part...until he
started involving his heart for real!*

PRETENDING WITH THE PLAYBOY
*by Cathleen Galitz
Coming to you from Silhouette Desire
In March 2003.*

*For a sneak peak,
Just turn the page!*

Prologue

"**S**orry, guys, no can do," Alexander Kent informed his fellow members of the prestigious Texas Cattleman's Club.

His voice lacked any genuine remorse at having to decline the "honor" thrust upon him. Protests arose from every corner of the ultra-manly cigar lounge that served as the day's meeting room. Clint Andover, the most recently married among their ranks, succinctly phrased the question on everyone's mind in a warm drawl that belied the steely intent behind the inquiry.

"And just why the hell not?"

Alex studied the fine-bone china cup that held his Irish coffee. The club emblem embossed in delicate gold strokes upon the porcelain stood for far more than any outsider could be expected to understand. The façade of their "good old boy" club was in fact a front for an organization of ex-military men dedicated to saving innocent lives and bringing the guilty to justice. And while their generosity to charities was renowned, it was their covert operations that truly testified to their members' integrity and to the success of their missions.

Alex took his sweet time answering. His gaze swept the room, taking in the exotic animal mounts decorating the walls. He felt a sudden stirring of empathy for the mountain lion trapped for posterity upon a narrow rock jutting out from the opposite wall. Swatting at an imaginary foe, the poor creature's snarl challenged the terrified look in its glassy eyes.

Alex imagined the unfortunate beast had just learned his friends had proposed marrying him off as part of some elaborate plan they had concocted on his behalf.

Overhead a Tiffany chandelier cast a rainbow of prisms upon the club motto hanging from a plaque above the door. The words were carved upon Alex's heart as surely as they were burned into that hallowed piece of wood.

"Leadership, Justice and Peace."

It wasn't lack of courage keeping Alex from freely offering himself up as a pawn in theC lub's latest mission. They intended to break apart a ring of white-collar criminals engaged in a reprehensible adoption scam. The scam had started coming to light on the fateful day when Natalie Perez stumbled into this proverbial fortress with Travis Whelan's baby— and absolutely no memory whatsoever. Piecing together her recollections had not been easy, or altogether safe, for those who had reached out to help her. And foiling a scheme worth a half a million dollars to the perpetrators had proven more perilous than any of them could have imagined at the time.

The fact that Natalie, Travis and their baby were presently out of harm's way, not to mention happily joined together as a bona fide family, wasn't the end of the Cattleman's involvement in this complicated case. Motivated by their pledge to see justice done, the members had seen fit to elect someone to go undercover and conduct a sting operation designed to put an end to the illegal ring for good. Because of his former FBI experience, Alex was the obvious choice for the assignment. Independently wealthy, this single thirty-five-year old lifetime bachelor had no family or job obligations to prevent him from accepting.

"We're waiting with bated breath," said Ryan Evans laconically.

Alex gave the former rodeo star a reluctant smile.

"As honored as I am by your faith in me, there's one problem you all seem to have overlooked."

He hesitated. The temptation to crack a joke and charm his way out of this predicament was superceded by his need to be forthright. Alexander Kent could no more lie to the reflection in his own mirror than to the band of brothers who filled this room with the integrity of their own personal character. Taking a deep breath, he removed the invisible mask of indifference that he donned for the rest of the world to see—and prepared himself to be razzed unmercifully.

A rare glimpse of weariness showed itself in his deep-green eyes as he made his disclosure.

"In order to play the doting husband in this little scheme of yours I'm going to need a suitable wife and, the truth is, I'm fresh out of female companions who would be willing to act the part—even for as good a cause as this one."

Disbelief and laughter filled the room at the thought of the state's most notorious playboy being unable to cajole any number of women into playing house with him.

"What happened to Glorious Gloria?" someone asked from the back of the room.

"Not speaking to me at the moment," Alex explained in reference to the supermodel who had recently severed ties when he refused to so much as discuss the subject of marriage. "As, I'm afraid, is every other woman in my infamous little black book."

The one that doesn't exist, he silently amended.

His friends' good-natured kidding didn't do anything to ease the loneliness that he secretly dealt with everyday as part of his inheritance from a wealthy father who had been taken by any number of rapacious stepmothers. Very early on those women had taught young Alex how to appreciate the value of bachelorhood. Gloria Vuu was the latest in a long line of women frustrated by their attempts to get him to commit to something beyond what they called his "swinging single's mind-set." Her dramatic departure had included the breaking of a priceless vase against a wall of his penthouse. Never one to quibble over the price of splitting up, Alex was just grateful she hadn't been a better aim.

"That one wouldn't have worked for our purposes anyway," interjected another friendly voice. "Nobody in their right mind would believe somebody like Gloria was desperate enough to saddle herself to a pile of dirty diapers."

With his usual aplomb, Ry Evans quieted the room simply by clearing his throat. "Is that all that's keeping you from accepting this assignment?" he asked, spearing Alex with a searching look.

As if that wasn't enough!

Alex nodded. Just because his bachelor friends were dropping like flies into the honeyed web of matrimony, he hardly thought it fair that they suddenly considered themselves experts on who would make him a suitable wife.

"If that's the case, I'm one step ahead of you, partner," Ry said with typical brashness.

The Cheshire grin his friend wore worried Alex.

As if afraid of being interrupted, Ryan continued

in a rush. "Since it's a given that none of the ladies you usually hang out with would provide you with a believable cover, I took the liberty of asking Carrie if she could think of someone who might fit the part. It just so happens that she has a friend who would be perfect marriage material for you."

Alex was just about to ask exactly what he meant by that when Travis interrupted his soon-to-be brother-in-law and longtime buddy. "If my little sister gives the lady the thumbs-up, that's good enough for me."

The set of his chiseled jaw dared anyone to question his judgment on the matter. Since Carrie had at one time been romantically involved with the doctor suspected of heading up this nefarious ring and who later turned on her with diabolical vengeance, there was no need to brief her on the need for utmost secrecy in regard to their plan. With both Travis and Ryan giving the mystery woman Carrie had picked out for him their seal of approval, no one else saw any reason to argue. Alex was morbidly curious to see just who Ry thought was the firecracker of a fiancée that would make him the perfect mate. If she was even half as pretty as Carrie, he knew he'd have a heck of a time staying focused on the business at hand.

The thought perked him up considerably.

"And just *who* might that be?" he wanted to know, mentally running through a list of available single women in town and crossing each and every one off as he came to them.

The name Ryan supplied had him picking his jaw up off the floor.

"The school librarian?" Alex asked in disbelief.

"One and the same. Before you object, you need to know that the lady not only has all the right understated qualities needed to actually pull this off, she's also got some acting experience under her belt."

Her chastity belt you mean, Alex was tempted to add.

Quite frankly, he was offended that Carrie would pick such a dowdy old maid as his "perfect" match. Not that Alex was one to fault a woman for living virtuously. If his own mother had shown more restraint than an alley cat before up and leaving her husband and five-year-old son high and dry, maybe he wouldn't be as emotionally screwed up as Gloria and an entire string of scorned women claimed he was.

On second thought, there were certain advantages to having such a plain Jane cast as his make-believe wife for this mission. Such a woman wasn't likely to come on board this project with any preconceived notions about becoming romantically attached to him, which would make it a whole lot easier for him to keep his focus. When dealing with dangerous criminals, the less distractions the better. As much as he would like to consider this assignment a lark, Alex understood just how perilous the game was they were playing. A man who would stoop to stealing babies from vulnerable single mothers wasn't likely to balk at murder.

Alex couldn't imagine the mild-mannered woman he had met at local school fund-raisers as being up to such a challenge. He doubted whether the demure Stephanie Firth would be willing to risk her previous reputation for a good cause, let alone actually risk her neck, by placing herself in the kind of compromising situations demanded by the plan Alex's friends had concocted with the two of them specially in mind.

Whatever threat such a plan posed to him personally, Alex would not turn his back on everything he held dear. The pledge he had taken as a Texas Cattleman precluded ever saying no to the friends who placed their trust in him. The thought of decent women like Natalie grieving for the babies they believe to be dead at birth demanded nothing less than laying his own life on the line if necessary.

Looking around the room at all the expectant faces turned toward him, Alex threw up his hands in surrender and put the onus on Miss Prim herself.

"All right, guys, if you think there's a chance in hell of convincing the little lady to go along with this, you're welcome to count me in."

You are about to enter the exclusive, masculine world of the...

The Stolen Baby

Silhouette Desire's powerful miniseries features six wealthy Texas bachelors—all members of the state's most prestigious club—who must unravel the mystery surrounding one tiny baby...and discover true love in the process!

ENTANGLED WITH A TEXAN by Sara Orwig
(Silhouette Desire #1547, November 2003)

LOCKED UP WITH A LAWMAN by Laura Wright
(Silhouette Desire #1553, December 2003)

REMEMBERING ONE WILD NIGHT by Kathie DeNosky
(Silhouette Desire #1559, January 2004)

BREATHLESS FOR THE BACHELOR by Cindy Gerard
(Silhouette Desire #1564, February 2004)

PRETENDING WITH THE PLAYBOY by Cathleen Galitz
(Silhouette Desire #1569, March 2004)

FIT FOR A SHEIKH by Kristi Gold
(Silhouette Desire #1576, April 2004)

Available at your favorite retail outlet.

Silhouette® Desire®

Looking for the mystery man at Mar Brisas Resort for another trip to heaven. Let's meet on the endless white sand for more pleasure in paradise. You can find it at Mar Brisas....
—The Lady in Blue

Nicole Whitaker had designed the billboard ad to bring in business to her dying hotel. But when her mystery man answers the ad, she gets a whole lot more than she bargained for!

Don't miss

Like a Hurricane
(Silhouette Desire #1572)
by

ROXANNE ST. CLAIRE

Available March 2004 at your favorite retail outlet.